A Not So
Model Home

Books by David James

THREE BEDROOMS, TWO BATHS, ONE VERY
DEAD CORPSE

A NOT SO MODEL HOME

Published by Kensington Publishing Corporation

A Not So Model Home

DAVID JAMES

KENSINGTON BOOKS
http://www.kensingtonbooks.com

KENSINGTON BOOKS are published by

Kensington Publishing Corp.
119 West 40th St.
New York, NY 10018

All Kensington titles, imprints and distributed lines are available at special quantity discounts for bulk purchases for sales promotion, premiums, fund-raising, educational or institutional use.

Special book excerpts or customized printings can also be created to fit specific needs. For details, write or phone the office of the Kensington Special Sales Manager: Kensington Publishing Corp., 119 West 40th St., New York, NY, 10018. Attn. Special Sales Department. Phone: 1-800-221-2647.

Kensington and the K logo Reg. U.S. Pat. & TM Off.

Library of Congress Control Number: 2012941702

ISBN-13: 978-0-7582-0632-9
ISBN-10: 0-7582-0632-1

First Hardcover Printing: November 2012

10 9 8 7 6 5 4 3 2 1

Printed in the United States of America

To Ann Stukas
Mother, and the greatest friend a son could ever have.
You will be forever missed.

A Not So
Model Home

CHAPTER I

The Cold, Hard Bitch Slap of Reality

We open on a woman sitting in a chair in a Spanish-style home living room. She is very beautiful and, contrary to popular opinion, does not look like Kathleen Turner punched in the face.

AMANDA: What have I learned from doing this reality show? Hmm... that you never know a person, even when you think you know them. And that people wear these masks that hide who they really are. You can never know if the person you are talking to, or trust, or love is a saint, a sinner, or a murderer.... *(There is a dramatic pause; then the woman continues.)* And that you have to remember that when you're saying good-bye to someone, you really are saying good-bye.

A single tear escapes her azure-frosted, luscious eyes and rolls down her porcelain skin. She blots her eyes with an unimaginably expensive handkerchief. She looks into the camera and we are struck by her intelligence, pathos, and beauty.

That's how I wanted it all to happen. But life doesn't always turn out that way. Two people were murdered. There was sabotage, incest, treachery, and the destruction of several expensive wigs. And we all came out smelling like something, but it was definitely not a rose.

Now, back to reality.

Regina Belle, my sexagenarian neighbor, and I are watching *The Cougars of Santa Barbara* at her house on a TV still housed in a Mediterranean-style faux-wood cabinet. This is not a nature documentary on the indigenous felines of California's Santa Ynez Mountains. No, this is a program about rich, bitchy, overindulgent women from the port city of Santa Barbara whose antics and bad behavior would put Paris Hilton to shame. Regina loves the program, and since I'm looking to get out and be more social, this fits the bill. Plus, her home is right next door, so it's within staggering distance after several blenders of tequila sunrises. Regina is wearing a new T-shirt sporting the phrase: BATTERIES NOT INCLUDED. SOME ASSEMBLY REQUIRED.

Me, I normally avoid reality shows precisely because there's so little reality in them. This is something that seems to escape most people. The dead giveaway is the fact that there always seems to be a camera ready to catch a tempestuous bitch storming out a door, or to be there at the exact moment an awkward meeting just so happens at a local restaurant. The other thing that gets me is that no one ever seems to flub a line when speaking. I can see the director asking for numerous retakes to get the line right, to capture the perfect pout or sneer. Let me tell you, life never works out that way. Because of my Catholic upbringing, I never have the ability to say the perfect comeback, packed full of venom like a pissed-off puff adder. Let me correct that last sentence. I *always* have the perfect comeback. Unfortunately, it comes to me three hours later, after I've stewed and fumed about a testy encounter and congratulated myself in not owning a gun. But it does no good to get in your car, drive over to the offending person's house, ring their doorbell, and let 'em have it. It's lost the impact, the immediacy; even if you top it all off with a biting bitch slap.

The weird thing about all these reality shows is they've turned the idea of a protagonist upside down. When I was a kid, you were supposed to look up to a show's main character. He or she was supposed to have redeeming characteristics. They were supposed to be smart, witty, sympathetic, kind, or at the very least, likable. Not anymore. You only rise to the top if you're vain, selfish, emotionally stunted, and above all, ready to act out for the cameras. Big time.

Regina, however, loves *The Cougars of Santa Barbara* for one reason only: "I love the fact that here are these vulgar, nouveau riche women horrifying the local Episcopalian stuck-ups with their antics," she would confess.

"Okay, Regina, how many times were you thrown out of Santa Barbara?"

"Twice," Regina replied.

"So *Cougars* is your revenge?"

"Partly. I also like the idea of owning a younger lover."

"Regina, from what I can see going in and out of your house, you have younger lovers."

"Amanda, I'm old—all my lovers are younger, comatose, or dead."

"Well, someone should call social services about some of these boys on *Cougars*. Some of them can't even be twenty-one."

"Amanda, the age of consent in California is eighteen."

"You seem rather sure about that."

"Knowledge is power," Regina smiled smugly.

"Knowledge that keeps you from being arrested."

"Exactly. So tell me, Amanda, what's wrong with women having all the power in a relationship for once?"

"Nothing, Regina. I applaud it wholeheartedly. But these women are paying for it."

"And what's wrong with that?"

"It's called prostitution, Regina."

Regina waved away my morals with a flip of her hand. "When I was working for Warner Brothers back in '53, I had a lot of the actors pay my way and no one gave it a second thought."

"But by becoming the paid-for girl, you lose your power in the relationship."

Regina was not to be outdone. "Women and men give up power all the time in a relationship."

"When?"

"Sex!"

"That's different, Regina. You wear that horse saddle willingly."

"Just like when you let Ken handcuff you to the bed."

"Touché, Regina."

Boy, you gotta be careful what you tell your friends. Ken, for the record, is a detective for the Palm Springs Police Department. Currently, we are seeing each other casually. Since we're both divorced, neither of us is intent on running into a new relationship. And furthermore, yes, I let Ken handcuff me to the bed while making love. You got a problem with that?

"But remember, Regina, this is a reality show," I said, putting vicious quotation marks around the word reality with two fingers on each hand. "There's very little that's real about it. I have a theory about these reality shows."

"Pray tell. What is it?" Regina asked, leaning forward to rest her head on her hand.

"It's the same thing as the early 1970s."

"The 1970s?"

"Yes, it was the rise of the ugly, of the unwashed masses rising up into popular culture."

"You sound like a snob."

"No, it's not that. Remember how ugly everything was in the early 1970s? The cars, the clothes, the hair, TV shows, architecture—everything. It's because the tastemakers were from the uneducated ranks."

"You still sound like an elitist," Regina commented.

"No, it's not like that. Vivienne Westwood, the British clothing designer, said that it's the role of art, of leaders, to set the pace, style, and manners by raising up the lower classes through good example."

"I would think she would be the last person you'd use as your barometer for good taste."

"Regina, you know what I mean. These reality shows reward acting out, bad, trendy clothes, selfishness, lack of consideration for others. It's similar to the 1970s. But now, it's vulgarity that's setting the levels of taste and human interaction."

"Look!" Regina exclaimed, turning away from my insightful observations of popular culture. "Jasmine just threw a cocktail in Heather's face! Someone's gonna get her earrings slapped clear off!"

"I rest my case," I relented as my cell phone rang. It was Ian Forbes, owner of a huge hair-care empire and a former client of mine. Perhaps it was much-needed business now that the second Great Depression was upon us.

"Ian, how nice to hear from you. . . . Yes, business is really slow . . . and how's yours? . . . No, not really . . . Well, that is a surprise. . . . I don't really think so . . . No, no, really, it's not my kind of thing. . . . How much? . . . Are you kidding me? . . . Are you sure? . . . Is this a joke? . . . No? . . . Okay . . . I'll consider it. Thanks for thinking of me. Okay, we'll talk more tomorrow. Bye."

Regina broke away from the fight brewing on the TV. "What was that all about?"

"You won't believe this, Regina, but I've just been invited to be on a reality show."

"A reality show?" Alex asked. "Go for it."

It was the next morning in the office and I had spilled the news to Alex, my ex-husband, soul mate, and still-business partner. We were married in Michigan years ago, moved here to Palm Springs, whereupon he confessed to me that he needed to be gay. I knew he was bisexual when I married him, but he was so handsome and exotic and from a family that wasn't highly dysfunctional like mine was, I jumped at his proposal of marriage. As it turns out, he needed a man, so we divorced amicably and we're still the best of friends. The trouble is, there's that soul-mate thing, too, blurring the line between friend and ex-husband/wife. It's complicated.

I was aghast.

"You heard me," Alex repeated himself.

"Why? You're the last person I would have predicted to say that."

"Amanda, times are tough. Like me, you have invest-ment properties you need to pay for, especially if you're taking cuts in rent just to keep them rented. And you still have some things you want to do to your house."

"Not too much. The house is almost finished."

"You've been at it for years, darling," Alex joked. "Your slow-as-molasses contractor finally moved out of the tent in your backyard last year."

I sniffed pompously. "A work of art is never finished . . . until you run out of money, which is kinda what happened to me."

"Well, then, go for it."

"I'm still trying to digest this."

"Listen, sweetie pie, besides making some money, you'll get notoriety, which could help publicize your—our—busi-ness. Plus, the show could go big time, and there might be book deals, spin-offs, and on and on. You could be famous."

"Alex, how could a show about a real-estate agent trying to sell a hairdresser's big Spanish house go big time?"

"It's a no-brainer. There's a big-time hairdresser involved who's vain, controlling, shallow, and prone to histrionics. And most likely, there will be good-looking men involved somewhere. The drama is a given."

"So you think I should do this?"

"Absolutely."

"You don't think this whole thing could backfire? That I get on the show and I end up looking like a self-absorbed, slut-bitch Realtor? These shows are looking for drama,

Alex. I can just see myself having an open house, with prospective buyers looking around the house, opening drawers and closets. Now that would make for riveting viewing. No, Alex, they're going to want people yelling at each other, throwing things, driving cars over the cherished possessions of rival cast members. This isn't going to be pretty."

"Okay, look on the bright side. Maybe someone will get murdered. If that doesn't get people to tune in, I don't know what will."

CHAPTER 2

An Indecent Proposal

The next day, I met Ian at his sprawling home in the Old Las Palmas neighborhood of Palm Springs. Ian's Spanish house is over 11,000 square feet, with eight bedrooms in three buildings on an acre of land. While that may not seem like a lot to those of you in Beverly Hills, or Bedford, New York, it's a lot for Palm Springs. Old Las Palmas is one of the oldest neighborhoods of Palm Springs, filled mostly with Spanish-style homes, some mid-century designs, and a scattering of modern styles. It's been home to Hollywood stars, captains of industry, and the women who married them. Now, it's mostly home to the dying descendants of those families or those who want to live in what is hands down the best area in town.

As I pulled through the gates (with Ian's initials, IF, boldly attached in fancy scripted, gold letters) and drove up the driveway to the house, my car was chased by a pack of wolves who surrounded my car when I stopped, barking endlessly as I made the decision against getting out of the car.

"Zeus! Hercules! Cut it out!. You . . . The rest of you . . . Get in the backyard!" a man shouted as the dogs cowered and started making their way back to hell, or wherever they came from. He was definitely leader of the pack.

He was an extraordinarily handsome man of about forty who looked as if he just stepped out of an Abercrombie & Fitch catalog. He approached my window and rapped on it with his knuckle. I powered the window down just enough to talk, but not enough for a dog to jump through.

"I'm Drake Whittemore, the property manager," the man said, squeezing his hand through the narrow slot for me to shake. I reached over with my right hand but slipped and ended up putting the window up, crushing his hand in the process. I quickly pressed the window button down, releasing his hand from the jaws of death.

"Damn!" he yelled, setting the dogs off in another frenzy of barking and unbridled excitement.

"Oh, my God, are you all right, Drake? I am sooooo sorry. Please forgive me," I added, getting out of the car and examining his hand, as if I knew what to do about a crushed hand.

"It's not too bad," he replied. "Come inside, Ian's been expecting you."

"I'm looking forward to it," I replied. "I know I can sell this house."

"Sell it?" Drake replied, giving me one of those boy-you-have-no-idea-what's-going-on looks. "Is that what Ian told you?" he said, shaking his head and chuckling.

I decided that this was one of those Linda Evangelista moments: just smile, look beautiful, and keep your mouth shut to keep from saying something stupid, a credo that supermodels should adhere to.

It was a perfect October day, very warm, but not hot. And topped by a cloudless sky so blue it could just make you cry.

The doors to the house stood open to the summer breeze that had just about disappeared everywhere else in the United States, but hung on here like the last guest to leave a party. As soon as I entered the house, I was accosted by a giant penis. I looked to the right: another penis, this time hanging from a sculpture on the wall. To the left, more penises. On the hall table, more penises. And around the living room, more penises, in paintings, more sculptures, water pitchers—you name it. And the one thing they all had in common was that they were large. Very large and pendulous. I wanted to pull a giant condom over my head. Ian had changed his décor again.

I'm not an expert in male homosexuality, having missed my ex-husband's desires even after he told me he was bi, but if you have to have penises all over your house in every form possible, you're not getting any. The other sign that you're sex-starved is that you're overweight. If you're not putting a cock in your mouth, you're shoveling food in it instead.

The house had changed since I was last here, at a party with me as the official fag hag. But then, if you had money like Ian had, you could afford to change it to suit your whims. It still had overtones of Spanish here and there, but it had taken a turn toward the dark side. Ian now had it decorated in Early Spanish Inquisition with a touch of monastic modernism. It was plain, simple, and with furniture that looked like it had been hewn out of old railroad ties, and on closer inspection, proved that my guess was probably right. I sniffed discreetly for the scent of creosote. The place dripped in forced masculinity, which was often the case with big ol' queens. It's not all taffeta, darlings.

"Ian, Amanda is here," Drake called up the stairway, reminding me how few homes had a second story in Palm Springs because of height restrictions. But this house had been built long before that. In fact, it had been lived in by many a silent film star—none of which I could prove because of a large fire in the town records building decades ago. I guess it didn't matter now to the Gen-X kids who were taking over the town. "Theda Bara who?" they'd ask. "Charlie Farrell? Who the hell is that!" they'd answer, taking a moment from their iPhones to text someone interconnected to the human race only by the safe skin of electronic transmissions. No human contact necessary. (Charlie Farrell, for whom Farrell Road is named, was part creator of the famous—infamous—Palm Springs Racquet Club, the lodging, swimming, and tennis club in north Palm Springs that helped put this town on the map. It attracted the biggest and brightest stars in the world at the time to Palm Springs, from Marilyn Monroe to Audrey Hepburn, from Joan Crawford to heiress Christina Onassis.)

A moment later, the biggest star in the world appeared: Ian. At the top of the stairs, he floated down in a cloud of not-so-subtly-perfumed hair, too long for the year 2012.

If you live in a cave and have never seen Ian on countless television programs burning the hair of annoying Hollywood celebrities, then let me describe him to you and let me tell you a little about his past.

Ian is the head of a ginormous hair-care products and salon empire. Some estimate that the entire net worth of his holdings tops $400 million. He wasn't always this wealthy or this well-known, however. Rising from very humble (dirt-poor) roots in Glasgow, Scotland, he had a salon there for a while and then immigrated to the United States a bazillion years ago. Well, while you can take the boy out of

Scotland, you can't take the itchy wool out of the boy. To capitalize on his Scottish heritage, to this very day he wears a kilt, works on his legs in the gym religiously (but sadly, not his stomach or his diet), and for some unknown reason, also wears a sort of headband to hold back his Braveheart mane. He rounds out the whole chic-and-trendy oddball appearance with large Jackie O sunglasses. Ian is the opposite of the masculinity he tries to project. Jewelry-wise, he's a cubic zirconium stone in a platinum setting.

"Darling," Ian gushed and planted an air kiss on both sides of my face. "Let me look at you!" He began fake crying. "Oh, Amanda, are you still letting that gobshite Micky Hamilton do your hair?" he added, forever in battle with his nearest rival, a local he could squash with one wave of his hand.

"Ian, you keep forgetting that Micky killed himself after you trashed his hair-coloring abilities on national television," I replied.

"And he couldn't even do that right. If I were to jump off a cliff, I would make sure it was high enough.

"Ian, it was over two hundred feet high."

"If you're going to kill yourself, you have to be thinking at least four to five hundred feet high. What you don't want to do is hit a bunch of rocks on the way down, bruising your face in case there are television cameras. You want to leap and make a huge splat and lie there on the ground, arms akimbo in a perfect swastika pattern for the photographers at the top of the cliff to capture. The aftermath is just as important as the act itself. Now, where were we? Would you like something to drink, Drake?" he asked into the air, but Drake had withdrawn from the room like an obsequious servant.

"No, thank you, Ian, it's a little early."

"It's ten o'clock! Perfect time for a hairball."

"A hairball?"

"That's what I call a highball around here."

"No thanks, Ian. So you want Alex and I to list your house?" I ventured, relishing the idea of listing one of the largest homes in Palm Springs.

Ian put an arm over my shoulder as he steered me toward his dining room. "Yes, but not right away."

"Rent it? We can handle that."

He stopped. "No, Amanda. As you know, a television producer wants to make a reality program here in my house."

"And I suppose it's a real-estate show?"

"Yes and no," he said, smiling like a crocodile waiting for an unsuspecting stork.

"It's going to be a reality show about finding an heir and boyfriend for me."

"A boyfriend, Ian? But you've had plenty over the years!"

"That's the problem, Amanda. Too many. I'm going to have my therapist, Aurora Cleft, as the judge on the program. We're going to bring back a handful of my present and former boyfriends onto the show and they're going to compete with each other, and Aurora is going to help me pick a suitable heir."

"Heir?" I snorted with a chuckle. "What, are you dying?"

"Unfortunately, yes."

I was horrified at what I had just said. Of course, not as horrified as the time I mistakenly uploaded a picture of myself making love with my ex-husband, Alex, to my real-estate Web site. Normally, this wouldn't be a big deal, but my Web site gets thousands of hits every month, so you can imagine my shock. And my continued shock when I found the very picture on several online sex galleries, including nymphouniverse.com.

"Oh, Ian, what's going on?" I asked with real concern in my voice—the first time such concern was probably ever uttered in his house.

"I have pancreatic cancer. Inoperable. So I might as well go out with a bloody great bang, huh?"

"So where do I come in?"

He looked around to make sure no one was listening, then walked me into the dining room where two men plainly from Los Angeles were sitting—you could tell from the heavy black Elvis Costello eyeglass frames they both wore.

Ian finished, "That's why I've invited these two gentlemen here—to discuss your role." He approached the dining room table and introduced the two men. "Amanda Thorne, this is Jeremy Collins and Tony Marcello. They're from the Q Channel."

"A pleasure to meet you," I uttered, extending my hand for them to shake as though it were a fragile lily. I threw in a curtsy.

"Perfect!" the man named Jeremy blurted out. "Ian, she's just what the show needs! A comic persona . . . some comic relief! And you were right about her offbeat looks! The nose too! Great! She does look like someone punched Kathleen Turner in the face!" he said. Then sideways out of his mouth, "Something I'd like to do myself to that haughty bitch!"

Jeremy was a tired, but prevalent stereotype from Hollywood. He seemed to speak mostly with exclamation points at the end of everything he said—like everything he said was brilliant. For Jeremy, excitement equaled believability. Tony motioned for me to sit down.

Jeremy continued, "I assume Ian's brought you up to date on the show! What we want to do with you is bring you in as a good friend. . . ."

"But I'm not Ian's *good* friend," I protested. "I guess that didn't come out right. He invites me to parties, he's a great client, but we don't see each other that often."

Jeremy laughed an ironic laugh. "Amanda, I know that. Ian's so toxic, he doesn't have any friends. You're like a . . . a stunt friend!"

"I don't have to do cartwheels while I'm on fire, do I?"

Jeremy mouthed to Ian: I love this woman! "No, what I meant is that you're a stand-in . . . since no one really likes Ian. Plus, you're a fag hag. . . . Gay viewers love fag hags."

Ian dabbed his eye with an imaginary handkerchief. "Now, Jeremy, let's not start with the testimonials right now. I'm not dead yet."

"You can bet you're not, Ian! You're going to be big! This series is going to be right up there with *American Idol!*"

Since I could remember, I have seen countless films, television clips, and read hundreds of novels that had characters like Jeremy in them, and I always felt that the characters were over-the-top, but necessary foils for the protagonists. But here in the flesh was the actual thing. If you could peel back the facade, you would find, well, nothing.

"So what do you want me to do, guys?"

Jeremy produced a thick document from seemingly nowhere and slid it across the table like a loaded gun in a game of Russian roulette. "Here's your contract, Amanda!

Read it, sign it, and get it back to us! Your primary role is that you're a good friend of Ian, and at some point, you get into your secondary role: to put Ian's house on the market! But you can't tell anyone else, including the others in the show, about putting the house up for sale! We're going to use it as a bombshell on the show, you know, to add the element of surprise! We've got to keep the drama up! It's *Survivor* crossed with *Project Runway* crossed with *The Real Housewives of Orange County*!" he said.

"Okay, Jeremy, I will go look over the contract and get back to you," I said, picking up the 100-page document.

Ian ushered me out of the room while Jeremy called from the background, "You're gonna be a star, Amanda! This opportunity is going to open doors for you everywhere. Doors you never dreamed existed."

Doors that I might get my fingers slammed in, I thought.

CHAPTER 3

Sign Now, Pay Later

"You ought to see this contract, Alex," I said, waving the thick document in the air. "It's worse than the amount of forms we have to fill out to sell a home. Sheesh. Listen to this, Alex, on page forty-five: 'Said participant, Amanda Thorne, shall not, at any time, hold liable . . . blah, blah, blah . . . for physical injury or trauma, miscarriage, nor for mental distress caused directly or indirectly by an appearance on *Things Are a Bit Iffy*.' "

"Wait a minute. The name of the show is *Things Are a Bit Iffy*?"

"Yeah," I replied, looking at Alex as if he had attacked me.

"Oh, I get it. The play off of Ian's initials: I.F. Clever."

"Well, I can tell you one thing. This contract is really making me think twice about being on the show."

"All contracts are like that, Amanda. Look at the ones we get from the banks once you have an accepted offer on a foreclosure house. The house you bought from us is built right on top of the San Andreas Fault line? Too bad. You should have talked to geologists first. The former owners poured cement down the drainpipes? You should have sent cameras down the sewage lines."

"So you don't think I should do this TV show?"

"On the contrary. I think it would build character. You'll build up a presence. You'll learn to speak on camera. You'll meet people. You'll make some money."

Make some money. Despite all the other reasons for being on the show, I think this is the one that stayed with me. We were still in the throes of the New Great Depression and I had exposure to several rental properties, none of which was fully rented. I needed cash, and the show was one way to bring in some money.

This Depression was like a speech being delivered by a presidential candidate—endless. It was all around us, but the real-estate agents were doing their best to hide it— even the ones with dozens of listings and a seemingly thriving business. You could see it in the clothes and the cars. You noticed that people were wearing the same outfits over and over—instead of tossing them into the trash after a few wearings when times were good. The cars said it all too. They were no longer sparkling clean every day of the week. Or, you noticed that they kept on being traded down, from top-of-the-line BMWs and Mercedes to the lower-end versions of the same models. Or worse, to Hyundais and Kias. When the mask falls off, it really makes a thud.

I went back into my office and signed the ominous paperwork, deciding once and for all to commit personal suicide and to stop worrying about it.

Then I had to get back to the business of selling homes in a market where no one was buying. I hunted Alex down and found him at the copier.

"I got another call from Angry Woman again. She wants to know why her house hasn't sold yet."

"Which Angry Woman? Be more specific."

"Mrs. Begley?"

Alex raised his splayed hands on either side of his head to express mock surprise.

"Did you tell her that her house is uglier than the south end of a northbound pig, it needs tens of thousands of dollars in repairs because she's either too lazy, cheap, or stupid to fix things when they start rotting, and it's overpriced by $200,000?"

I shook my head.

"I told her that you and I *work* in the market. We don't *control* it," I said.

"To which she responded . . ."

"She said she wants to see her house on television. She thinks this whole Internet thing is a fad and TV is the way to go."

"Amanda, we explained that to Mrs. Begley. Close to ninety percent of all people look for homes on the Internet. Local media is only for those agents to trumpet their listing and get more of them. Those ads don't sell homes."

"She said she wants to see her home on *The Tonight Show*. She likes Leno."

"Let me tell you what, Amanda. Let's just get rid of all the overpriced listings and all the fucked-up sellers."

"Then we wouldn't have any homes for sale, Alex."

"That's not true, Amanda. What about James Murray? His home is mid-century, it's priced right, it looks great."

"The last agent who showed it said there were one hundred twenty rifles stacked in the closet and that there was a six-month supply of food, water, and ammunition in the garage."

"So the guy likes to hunt, Amanda. . . . And hydrate often. What about Janis Frommer?"

21

"She shot her husband in the face with buckshot on the front lawn of her home after she found him in bed with her sister."

"She has anger-management issues. So what?"

"Alex, I know you are fed up with all the shit in this business. Me too. This used to be a pleasant business to be in. You took people around, they found a nice home, they went to get a loan and got it without threatening anyone, and the house sold and we got paid. Now, it's like a hatchet fight with the two opponents handcuffed to each other."

"I think it's more like *Who's Afraid of Virginia Woolf?* Week after week."

"I have had just about as much as I can take. The sellers think they're sitting on a pile of gold and that they're in the driver's seat, and when someone is stupid enough to put a full-price offer on a home, then we can't make the appraisal and the whole deal falls apart and the seller yanks the listing from you after you've spent all this time and money, only to give it to another agent who's desperate to have a listing under his or her belt."

"That's it in a nutshell, Amanda. The sellers are unrealistic and haven't come to the reality that their house is worth a lot less than they paid for it. Then along comes an agent who's terrified that he or she has another car and mortgage payment due, and that they don't want to be known as the agent with no listings, so they take the overpriced listing and the abuse that follows while the agent tries to ratchet them down into reality adjacent. It's a vicious cycle."

"Like buying panty hose."

"Exactly."

I looked into Alex's eyes.

"I think we should become door-to-door dildo salespeople. We would probably make more money."

"And we'd have a lot more fun."

"How's about it, Alex? I said, offering my hand to shake and close the deal.

"I'm in."

CHAPTER 4

Let the Games Begin

A week later, the initial cast meeting for *Things Are a Bit Iffy* was called at Ian's house at 9 A.M. When I arrived at Ian's estate, I was surprised to see no camera crews or large semi-trucks filled with cameras and lighting equipment.

The parking area to Ian's house is very large and usually filled with unimaginably expensive cars—all Ian's. But today was different. The cast was here to snag an enormously, fabulously wealthy boyfriend, so the parking lot was full of gleaming, top-of-the-line Mercedes, BMWs, a Rolls Royce, and one Lamborghini—all probably rented. I assumed that one or two of the cars belonged to the show's producers and directors, but the rest were all for show. And what a show it was. I almost felt ashamed to park my Toyota Land Cruiser next to such ultimate driving machines.

I climbed the stairs to the living room to find it full of gay men who were as gleaming and polished as the cars they supposedly owned. Gucci and Prada shoes, $400 jeans, tailored long-sleeve shirts with cuff links—these guys all had the looks down pat. Except one. A short, steroidal muscleman with tattoos visible even on his neck stood there in the crowd of peacocks looking as out of place as myself. Me, I was dressed in casual chic, but that's not why I stood out. I was the only woman in a sea of gay men.

There were plates of deftly arranged breakfast foods that made me drool, but I quickly noticed that none of the men were eating. They all had very European, emaciated figures, and they intended to keep them, especially now that flat-fronted pants were all the rage. Of course, this didn't stop Mr. Musclehead. He shoveled in the protein while steering clear of the carbs.

The thought struck me. Unless this was some kind of colossal joke on Ian's part, there was a phenomenal amount of money at stake. Millions! These guys were dressed to kill, and to get their hands on that much, it occurred to me that someone just might.

Jeremy Collins, the producer, clapped his hands several times in rapid succession to call us to order.

"Welcome, everyone, thanks for agreeing to be on *Things Are a Bit Iffy*, one of the biggest reality-show hits of the '12 and '13 season!"

Again with the exclamation points. I pictured Jeremy—if he was lucky to have landed a boyfriend who could stand his never-ending hype—at home over morning coffee, gushing over a strawberry Pop-Tart. This would be followed by a breathless description of his morning bowel movement and a recounting of the amazing dreams he had last night that no one, mind you, no one could top in their vividness. Of course, as improbable as it would seem, Jeremy would have no trouble locating a partner who could stand him. There's always a man willing to put up with endless bullshit in order to have a cushy life. And a cushy life is something that Jeremy's endless string of Aaron Spelling-inspired television bilge probably provided.

"Let's go into the dining room and we'll talk about the show and what we can all do to make it the hit of the season!"

The guys filed in with a veneer of civility, but you could see the tiny, imperceptible sprint that shot into their steps in order to secure a chair near where they figured Ian would sit—at the head of the table, naturally. Then, within seconds after entering the room, you could see the faces fall like so many shoddy apartment buildings in a Chinese earthquake. There were place cards on the table indicating where everyone should sit. Based on the slight mouth movements, you could tell there was a chorus of "shits" being uttered at frequencies only dogs could hear. Once everyone was seated, the show began. Once, that is, Ian took his seat. Everyone managed to flash a smile at Ian and score a point or two, depending on the whiteness of their teeth. The sets of choppers on some of the guys were so white they could have starred on episodes of *Baywatch*. My porcelain toilet should shine so brilliantly.

Jeremy began, "I'd again like to welcome you all to the show. Let me tell you a little about the concept of the show and the arc we hope to follow." This comment fell on a sea of blank stares. Jeremy, ever in a world of his own making, continued unabated, "But before we begin, Ian would like to have his spiritual advisor bless our undertaking. Ian?" he said, giving way to Ian with the wave of his hand.

"Thank you. As some of you know, I am a very, very spiritual man," he said, holding up the string of black wooden beads he was wearing around his neck this morning as proof. "So I have asked my spiritual guru, the Sai Baba Shu Baba, to bless us as we begin this remarkable journey today. Several of the guys rolled their eyes, no doubt familiar with

Ian's whirlybird spiritual explorations that were pounced on as soon as they became fashionable, then discarded just as quickly as last season's Dolce & Gabbana. Buddhism, Cabala, Scientology, Mayan. In one day, out the next.

From behind a curtain emerged a man dressed in an orange Nehru-collared silky shirt with an enormous Afro. He looked like an Indian Phil Spector—without the guns. His face was henna-decorated with supposedly mystical symbols, one of which looked awfully close to a dollar symbol. He stood and raised his hands as if to welcome his gathered faithful. Ian actually got up from his chair where he held court in order to prostrate himself and kiss the guru's Gucci loafers. (I noticed, since my ex had a pair just like them.) This was probably the first time that the people present had ever seen Ian humble himself.

The guru or swami or whatever he was began talking in a foreign language, chuckled to himself several times, raised his arms up toward the ceiling a lot, then departed.

The man who was sitting next to me whispered in my ear, "That little charade will cost Ian $5,000, plus travel expenses."

"I'm in the wrong business," I whispered back.

"I'm David."

"Amanda here," I said, offering my hand to shake.

Ian was trying hard to appear that he was at peace, closing his eyes and holding the palms of his hands skyward. "You may continue, Jeremy."

"The show, the show . . ." Jeremy mused. "Think of a cross between *The Real Housewives of Orange County* and *Top Chef*! It's a slice-of-life reality show and a competitive show at the same time—a powerful hybrid. The show is what we in the industry call soft scripted. That means it's not written by costly and temperamental members of the Writers Guild of America. Instead, we have a loose plan of where we want the arc of the show to go, and on each episode, we have a loose plan where we might suggest certain actions we would like each cast member to take based on what happened on the previous episode or earlier in a day of shooting!"

I thought to myself, *They're going to make it up as they go along and convince everyone within earshot that what they're doing is brilliant and spontaneous.*

Jeremy continued, "Each day, we'll be shooting with handheld cameras at some sort of event, such as a pool party for the first episode, or a dinner, for example, and based on what happens during each two- or three-hour shoot, we'll pull you contestants aside to do an interview to give viewers some insight into your more private thoughts and reactions!"

A hand went up.

"Yes, Gilles?"

"I do not understand."

"Okay, let's say that during a pool party, Keith calls you a snotty piece of self-absorbed Eurotrash. Maybe he says it to your face, or he says it on camera during the shooting, but you're not in attendance at the time he says it. Well, after we shoot a few hours, we'll recap what we got and tell you that Keith called you a gold-digging piece of Eurotrash. Then you'll be shot alone, sitting, I don't know, in a pool chair, in which you can respond, saying you are hurt by his comment, and then you might make a comment about his appalling lack of personal hygiene."

"So ve have ze everyday, reality part, zen the interview?"

"In a nutshell, that's pretty much it. Then the shoots all

go to the editors and they put it together, and voilà, we have an episode. Before the next episode, we all sit down and watch the previous episode of rough cuts again so it's clear where we want the trajectory of the next program to go. All the while, Aurora and Ian react to what's going on. And in the final show, we announce the winner, and that man becomes Ian's boyfriend and heir to a substantial portion of Ian's personal money. Now, as you've seen in the legal papers we asked you gentlemen to sign, the winner immediately receives $15 million to be held in a trust account until Ian's demise, which will be monitored by Lance Greenly, Ian's CEO. You're free to spend the $15 million. Upon Ian's demise, another $57 million will pass to the winner."

"Who's Aurora?" someone asked.

"Ian's psychiatrist, therapist, whatever," Jeremy replied. "And mine. She's the one who selected you from a list of previous boyfriends that Ian drew up."

"So, ze winner marries Ian and gets a lot of money?" Gilles asked.

"What we're looking for is a suitable partner for Ian, since he is dying."

You would have expected a round of gasps, but there were none. I swear to God, I thought I saw faint smiles on several of the faces gathered around the table. This was followed by a sudden burst of faked concern for Ian, which he accepted with a wave of his hand like a Pope accepting well wishes from the faithful in St. Peter's Square.

"Yes, Ian is dying of pancreatic cancer, but let's not get off track here or get mired in all the little details! What we have to remember is that this will be a first in television history! *The Bachelorette* has the promise of love. *Dancing with the Stars* can give the winners big-time recognition and fame. This show has DEATH! And MONEY. Fuck *Sur-vivor*! This is going to make *American Idol* look like *Mr. Rogers*! This is big, Big, BIG!"

Gilles spoke up. "I dun't knew why ve have to go on viss dis charade? Ian was in love with me until chose zeese, how do you say, skanky ho zitting next to me," he said, pointing to Keith (his name card said).

I had to give credit to Gilles. He pronounced one somewhat-current American phrase completely right and without an accent.

The fur was beginning to fly already and we'd just barely started.

The skanky ho seated next to Gilles spoke. "I think that we should try and keep this civil, no matter how much of a piece of Eurotrash we are."

Gilles reacted in a typically French manner. I half expected sabers to be drawn. Gloves to be struck across startled faces. Hair being pulled and eyes being scratched.

"Is he inzulting me?"

This time it was Jeremy who was licking his lips. Already, the mix of men here was explosive. Helen Keller could see it.

Jeremy said, "Fellows, let's save this for the show, although you are getting the hang of it. Drama! But let me get back to the meat of the matter. So, we will film this series mainly here in this house, and occasionally around town. Basically, the show is a contest. Aurora Cleft will be here starting at the first episode. She and Ian will see how you handle different situations, answer questions, and how you live your everyday life. But never forget, this show will fail or succeed on the kind of drama you give me and your best friend, the camera. Just remember, at the end of the show, the winner could be a titanically rich man!"

Ian coughed ever so slightly.

"Oh, and the winner will also have the love and companionship of Ian!" Jeremy finished, then added, "Ian wants to spend his last days with a loving partner."

You could feel the disappointment in the room from this realization. It was like being awed by a stunt plane doing figure eights in the sky, which then suddenly plunged into an open field. This offer had a big and paunchy string attached to it.

"Oh, one last thing," Jeremy added. "We are promoting the hell out of this show both on Q Channel and the Internet. YouTube, Twitter, Yahoo trending, celebrity Web sites! You won't be able to turn on a computer and not see something that has to do with *Things Are a Bit Iffy*."

All the contestants flashed toothy grins, while some tossed smoochy air kisses Ian's way. It was clear that the men sitting around the table would have no problem with the money part, but having Ian thrown in with the deal was a problem that would have to be tolerated until a quick death solved everything. I sat there stunned, thinking that a reality show was going to decide how a certain man at this table was going to inherit more money than any of us could probably ever spend.

"Now, since we don't all know each other, I think we should go around the table and introduce ourselves, tell us a little about you . . . starting with you, Drake."

"Hi, I'm Drake Whittemore. I'm Ian's property manager. I was born and raised in Darien, Connecticut. I'm thirty-five. I graduated from Yale. I'm a world-class technical mountain climber, up to 5.10c. I've climbed Mount McKinley in Alaska; I placed in the Olympics rowing trials; I've placed in the top final heat scores at the ASP World Surfing

Tour, the Billabong Pipeline Masters in Oahu and Tahiti, the Quiksilver Big Wave Competition, and the O'Neill Surfing World Cup; I work out five days a week at the gym; and volunteer time helping autistic children. I guess that's all."

Drake had effectively let the air out of the men in the room. A pair of Dries Van Noten pants and Gucci-clad feet weren't going to score a lot of points right now. Drake was everything the other men were not: masculine, honest, and smart. He didn't have the Euro-sleek look of the other men; but make no mistake, he was strikingly handsome in a wholesome, all-American way. His predatory looks, dark hair, eyebrows that sat overshadowing deep-set eyes and slanted downward in a straight line toward the nose, and prominent, chiseled jaw gave him both a smoldering and somewhat dangerous—shall I say, almost sinister in a sexy way—look. He could have walked right out of an early Ralph Lauren Polo ad.

All eyes went to the next man at the table, Mr. Frenchy.

"I ham Gilles Moreau, I ham six feet tall . . . and eleven inches," he said with a not-so-subtle wink.

Since we were seated, it was difficult to ascertain how tall anyone was, but it was clear what Gilles was hinting at. Plain and simple, Gilles was cute Eurotrash with a big dick, and apparently a desire to get his hands on a lot of money. He had longish black hair as thick as the bristles of a shoe brush, swept back and up from his face, as if he lived life in a wind tunnel filled with hair spray. His two lips were permanently pursed into a perfect heart shape at the middle, revealing two beaver-like incisors that forced his lips to part in a tempting look of come hither. He had no brutish jaw like Drake. It simply eased back to disappear into his swan-like neck as if it wanted to slip away gracefully, unnoticed.

Even though he was male, he had this light, gossamer overlay of femininity.

Gilles continued, "And I am so qualified to be the boyfriend of Ian, I sink zere is no reason for the others to stay! I win!" Gilles laughed . . . all by himself. What might have been a knee-slapper in Paris landed like the carcass of a deer on the table. You could smell the contempt in the room.

Jeremy spoke up, "Anything else, Gilles?"

"No, ze contest is over. I am ze best."

A very satisfied smile rose in the corners of Jeremy's face. Gilles was just the match to throw into the ammunition pile. Arrogant. Narcissistic. Sociopathic. "Very well, then, Gilles. Next?"

"I am Aleksei Kikorov. Big surprise: I am a fashion model. I'm currently taking a break from a busy career here in Ian's house," he reported dryly without a hint of an accent of any kind—despite the exotic name.

Gilles was not done talking. "You forgot to zay zat you are a kree-stal meth head in rehab here."

"I have nothing to hide. I have been clean for six months now."

"Seeex months! They always go back to ze drugs," Gilles added.

"Gilles, could you just shut that sewer that you call a mouth for one goddamned minute?" Keith MacGregor (name card again) said as he was texting from his Black-Berry phone, not bothering to look up. "Unlike others, I will wait my turn to talk," he added, raising his eyebrows in unison and nodding his head slightly in the direction of Mr. Eurotrash. "Continue, Aleksei."

Aleksei continued, "Gilles, I've spent sixty days in rehab," he retorted snottily while taking a rather large gulp of wine. "I'm clean."

What wine was doing at a breakfast table was a mystery to me, but I did notice that Aleksei was the only one with it in front of him. To be fair to Aleksei, the others merely had Bloody Marys. Alcohol was apparently the one acceptable carb.

"So you drink ze wine now?"

Raised eyebrows from a few guys and some dagger eyes from Keith.

"I was at Beginnings in Malibu for substance abuse. I'm sure you've all heard of it. All the big stars have gone there. Charlie Sheen, I think. Anna Nicole Smith went there. I'm clean now. Wine doesn't count."

"Even zo, you like your wine. I saut zat you go there to stop drinking too?"

"That was for hard liquor. Wine is different. This is California. You get arrested for not drinking wine. Plus, it's good for your arteries. Keeps them open or something to do with trans fatty acids. How should I know, I'm not a chemist."

"I vould zink you know a lot about ze chemicals, Aleksei," Gilles said, getting in one last dig.

Aleksei raised his nose in the air. "I will not dignify that comment. That's about it. Ian has been very good to me."

Gilles replied, "I'll bet he has."

"Always trying to have the last word, aren't you, Gilles?"

Aleksei was young. I was guessing about twenty, if that. Like any man who attracted Ian's eye, he was abnormally handsome. Again, we had the huge-hair syndrome, but his was swept upward in a single, light brown wave that made him look like a Russian James Dean. And again, the lips—perfectly pursed. It finally occurred to me how many of them had collagen injections in their lips. Everything was all too perfect, too structured. But if you looked a little closer, you could see that Aleksei was already showing huge amounts of wear and tear from the crystal meth. His cheeks were almost imperceptibly sunken, the face a tiny bit shriveled, and he had a jumpiness that showed up in tapping fingers, restless feet, and gazing around nonstop. He couldn't stop fidgeting in his chair, and his hands were fluttering like a pair of Monarch butterflies on their way back from Mexico for the winter.

Gilles was about to lob out another verbal cluster bomb when Keith raised his hand to silence him—again, without looking up from his over-texted BlackBerry. Oddly enough, when I thought even a volcanic eruption couldn't stop Gilles from talking, Keith's hand had calmed the waters temporarily.

Jeremy motioned for Keith to talk next.

"I'm Keith MacGregor. I'm an event planner, nightclub promoter, and bulk texting expert in Los Angeles."

This pronouncement was met with blank stares all around the table.

"I help build, design, and promote cutting-edge nightclubs in Los Angeles. Like Area, the Skybar, Element."

"You had nothing to do with any of soze clubs," Gilles chimed in again, giving the shit pot another good stir.

"I said I build and design nightclubs like them. I didn't say those clubs exactly. I am very much involved in the design of Water, Tube, and Sonic," Keith replied with a bit of cocky bravura.

"I figure as much," Gilles added. "No wonder nobody goes to soze clubs."

Keith looked up at Gilles like a dog about to attack. Head

lowered, eyes glowing like red coals looking up at you from beneath hostile brows. Then he smiled, poured himself some more cranberry juice, took a long drink, and was quiet. Keith's appearance? Not like the rest. Instead of the polished, sleek look of most of the others, Keith looked, well, disheveled. Between the wild, longish hair, the beard stubble, and the dark circles around the eyes, he looked like a vampire who partied way too much. Jeremy was right—Keith looked like personal hygiene and grooming took a back seat to everything else in his life.

Aleksei reached for his wineglass again, which I noticed had been magically refilled. His grasp slipped and the glass tipped over on the table, spilling the contents.

Ian broke in, "Drake, would you be a dear and mop up Aleksei's spill?"

Drake got up with just a hint of frustration on his face, picked up the glass, mopped up the spill, and headed for the kitchen.

"Drake, where are you going, boy?" Ian sneered with a barrelful of attitude.

"What? The glass is chipped. I'm throwing it away, Ian!"

"Let me see that glass," Ian demanded.

He studied the glass, turning it this way and that. He then put on his reading glasses that hung on a jeweled chain around his neck.

"I don't see anything, Drake."

Drake let out a sigh that could've woken the dead.

"Right there, Ian!" he said, pointing to an area on the rim.

"My God, Drake! You'd have to have the Hubble telescope to see that chip. Okay, throw it away, Drake. You win!"

Drake left the room and went into the kitchen, where we were treated to the sound of the glass being thrown at great velocity against a wall, shattering into a million pieces. This followed by what sounded like someone kicking in the side of an aluminum pizza pan.

"The way that man spends my money!" Ian complained.

"David," Jeremy said, moving things along, "would you like to introduce yourself? Tell us a little about you."

Gilles was about to let loose another volley when Aleksei clapped a hand over Gilles's mouth. It worked!

"I'm David Laurant." Like the others, he was abnormally handsome in a young, waif kind of way. But David had a different kind of look. His hair was dyed a bright white and was spiked up, and between the hair and the oversized Tom Ford tortoiseshell horn-rim glasses that made up most of his face, he had a constant look of being surprised. His eyes were bright and mischievous. I could tell right from the start he was going to be bubbly, energetic, and a whole lot of entertainment and drama. But not a lot of substance. And I was not disappointed.

"I've modeled since I was sixteen for Armani, Gucci, Tom Ford, and I was the lead model at Alberto Garelli's 2006 Hobo Show."

"*That* show set the standard. Fabulous!" Aleksei said with a didactic seriousness.

"I know, wasn't it?" David agreed. "The show director said I actually looked like I had tuberculosis. That's how I got to be the opening *and* closing model. They don't have shows like that anymore!"

"Having the models crawl out of cardboard boxes at the beginning and the end of the show . . . totally brilliant!" Aleksei relished.

"The press was really unkind to Alberto because of that show," David defended. "Everyone is so PC nowadays. You can't even make fun of the homeless anymore. I personally have nothing against them, but if they didn't smell like sour milk . . . Hey, I have an idea. Perfume for the homeless! Genius! I thought of it first," David added, then pulled out his iPhone and began texting his million-dollar idea to what I presumed was his good friend, Karl Lagerfeld.

"Is there anything else that you'd like to tell us about yourself, David?" Jeremy plied.

"No, I'm a very in-demand model. What else can there be worth telling?"

Then we came to the square peg in the round hole: Marcus Blade. Marcus was the complete opposite of everyone at the table. Unlike the skinny, androgynous physiques that made the other men into perfect, human clothes hangers, Marcus was built like a brick shithouse, his body so puffed up by steroids that he looked like an overstuffed knockwurst engorged with blood. He was short, too: a sapling in this forest of redwoods. I managed to get a good look at him when we were milling about earlier and he couldn't have been much taller than five feet six inches. He didn't even attempt to squeeze himself into the fine European clothing the other guys were sporting. Oh no, little Marcus had obviously spent much of his life in the gym and he wanted us to be sure of that fact, with a T-shirt stretched so tight you could actually see his abdominal muscles through it: a rare eight-pack. I counted. The other models probably had visible abdominal muscles, too, but there's a difference between those created from strenuous crunches and those induced by frequent bulimic vomiting.

"I'm Marcus Blade. Most of you know me. I'm Ian's personal trainer."

There was a violent fit of coughing around the table. One look at Ian's blubbery body and it was clear that either Marcus was a miserable failure as a trainer or he was Ian's stud. I guessed the latter. The participants around the table looked at Marcus, expecting more, but nothing came. There were some whisperings about his height, followed by some tittering. I guess that was it for Marcus. He was obviously paid to screw Ian and didn't care to pretend that he was anything else. At least he was honest.

Jeremy then turned to me. "Amanda here," he explained, "is Ian's good friend."

This comment got even blanker stares from the contestants than Keith's comment about being a bulk texter. There were a few disbelieving snorts, and no wonder. Those close enough to Ian would know that Jeremy's proclamation was patently false, and those who were just bedmates for Ian probably didn't give a shit. I was a woman and, therefore, no threat. Of course, I could have explained that I was a Realtor there to eventually list Ian's house for sale, but I was forbidden by contract to let on to this fact. The smarter boys would no doubt go online and in 2.5 nanoseconds, figure out that I was a real-estate agent, and know instantly what I was there for. These boys probably couldn't discuss Cartesian metaphysical and epistemological principles, but you could bet that they could figure out when there was a threat to their financial well-being.

"Yes, I've been best friends with Sean for years," I said, making my first big faux pas.

"You mean Ian," Aleksei corrected me like a tired schoolteacher giving the answer to a simple question to a dumb student.

"Ian. Yes."

"I know how easy eet eez to call out zomeome else's name," Gilles retorted, jumping right in. "Especially during sex. I hear that Aleksei does it all the time when he's with Ian."

While everyone was incensed with the way Gilles ceaselessly lobbed flat-footed insults like show-me-your-breasts Mardi Gras beads, Ian seemed to cherish the tussles that he instigated. Ian, it was clear, thrived on conflict and liked being fought over.

Jeremy attempted to wrap things up. "Now zat we all know each other . . ."

"No, we don't," Gilles spoke up. "Who's zat?" he asked, pointing at a rather plain-looking, middle-aged man standing off to one side of the dining room.

"That's Lance Greenly," Ian explained. He's my CEO and business manager for my hair-products empire. You've met him a dozen times. He comes here all the time on business."

More blank stares.

It was becoming clear that unless you were muscled or handsome, you didn't register here. At all.

Don't get me wrong, Lance wasn't ugly by a long shot. But being surrounded by these abnormally handsome men was enough to make George Clooney look like a skank. Lance must have been around forty, with a receding hairline that he wisely kept short. He had a long, drawn-down face with a heavy five-o'clock shadow and red eyes that made him look like he had been crying for decades. I guessed he was about five feet eight. Lance, working for a style Nazi like Ian, dressed very, very well, but he didn't stand a chance in this room of mannequins. Like the attitude of the boys at the table, whose motto surely had to be "amaze me or I will dismiss you," Lance was probably cast off long ago due to his lackluster appearance and his terrifying potential to use scary and hard-to-understand corporate terms that could upset the guys now sitting at the table.

Tony Marcello, Jeremy's silent servant, tiptoed up to Jeremy, whispered in Jeremy's ear, then departed the room walking backward like a peasant in King Henry's court.

"Well, we were going to save this surprise for later, but Ian's therapist, Aurora Cleft, is here in town a few days ahead of schedule. We might as well have her come in and introduce herself," Jeremy said, waiting for our surprise guest to appear.

A minute later, she entered the room and clattered across the soft pine floors on heels so tall, they pumped her petite frame up almost five inches. The soles of the shoes were a bright red: Christian Louboutin. Though she was very small, she walked with an intensity that suggested that very little would stand in her way, and anyone who did would end up like flattened roadkill. She dressed in a voluminous black knitted dress cinched tightly around her wasp-waist with a huge black belt. She wore black tights that completely covered her legs. She looked like a female superhero: Black Spandex Woman. In contrast with her preference for dark clothing, her hair was shocking Annie Lennox white, parted severely in on the right side of her head, with the left part perpetually covering her left eye like an eye patch. I suppose in parts of Los Angeles this was supposed to be fashionable, but to me, it looked sinister—an effect that probably wasn't lost on Aurora. If she were suddenly thrust into a fashionable woman's prison, Aurora would be nobody's bitch.

Aurora didn't take a seat at the table even though there was a chair open for her. Instead, she leaned forward and placed her widely spaced hands (with talon-like fingernails, painted black) firmly on the table as if to remind a reluctant board meeting that she was in charge.

"I'm sure Jeremy introduced me already, but just in case he hasn't, I'm Aurora Cleft. I am Ian's psychiatrist, and I'm here on the show as a relationship counselor, to help him choose a suitable boyfriend—and heir. I've had a very successful practice in Los Angeles for over a decade, and I've treated some of the biggest names in Hollywood. I can't tell you who they are because of therapist–patient confidentiality, but believe me, I'm talking big names. I've written several books you might have read"—she looked at the empty-headed expressions on the faces at the table—"or heard of: *Kick Your Own Ass*; *You're Not a Victim . . . Just a Pathetic Wimp*; and *Lonely? Get Over It!* I believe in the individual taking charge of his life and not whining a lot about it. I'm tough, I'm smart, and I don't suffer bullshit. Okay, gentlemen, let's go make history, let's get ratings, and good luck to all of you. Some of you are going to need it," she finished, looking squarely at Gilles.

I didn't know whether to clap or storm the beaches of Normandy. I didn't know what to think of Aurora. Yes, I did. I thought she was a bitch.

Gilles, true to his nature, made a mumbling comment about Aurora's being "vertically challenged." I'm surprised Gilles would know a word that was so, well, American.

Aurora's head spun in Gilles's direction so quickly I thought

I was going to hear neck bones cracking. "When Katharine Hepburn first met Spencer Tracy, she was wearing high heels and commented that maybe she was a bit tall for him, to which he responded, 'Don't worry, I'll cut you down to size.' I may be short, Gilles, but don't forget that I am here to make sure Ian finds a suitable partner who thinks with more than his dick. I've seen your type before."

Boy, I wish the cameras were rolling just then. That would have made a Kodak moment. Aurora had shut up Gilles for the time being.

Suddenly, I liked Aurora a lot more. She was starting to grow on me.

Jeremy jumped in like a trendy ringmaster. "Well, that's the cast! You all know each other. When we start filming on Monday, the context will be a pool party here at Ian's house. I want to you to arrive in street clothes, but bring sexy swimsuits to wear for the party. . . . That means you, too, Amanda—I plan on having a lot of lesbians following this show too. That means a Brazilian wax," Jeremy announced, pulling an imaginary strip of waxed pubic hair from his crotch with a ferocious jerk of his arm. "For those of you who could use a little touching up on the tans, I'd spend a few hours brushing up over the weekend . . . but don't overdo it. And please hit the gym as much as you can. I want you all looking sexy, pumped, groomed, and with bulges in your swimsuits. There will be several cameras roving around, taking down your every word, so if you're going to say something to the camera, be yourselves . . . but be nasty. I want conflict, I want competition, I want men here wanting to win. I want big ratings."

I raised my hand timidly.

"Yes, Amanda?"

"As Ian's long-time friend, what is my role exactly?"

"To be his friend."

"I know that, but how am I supposed to interact with these gentlemen?" I trailed off.

"Just be yourself, Amanda. Do what friends do. Comfort Ian . . . er, look, Amanda, I'm a producer. Everyone hates me. What would I know about friendships? In my business, you befriend someone and they stab you in the back, wipe their shoes on you, then climb over your lifeless body. That's why I have no friends; can't trust 'em in Hollywood. Plus, I'm a driven, obnoxious, toxic person. Who in their right mind would want to be my friend?"

There was no argument there. I didn't know how to answer him. Jeremy was so stereotypically narcissistic that if I called him what he really was—a total dickhead—it would bounce off his protective exterior without so much as a dent. I decided to stick with what manners my mother taught me: If you don't have anything nice to say about someone, say it behind their back.

"I guess I'll make sniping and bitchy comments about the other contestants, have others give me the finger, duck when someone throws a wineglass at my head, and get swept up in what promises to be a tsunami of self-manufactured and unnecessary drama. You know, like what happens on a typical realty show."

Jeremy clapped his hands, the twenty-odd, trendy silver bracelets on his left arm jingling like a slot machine jackpot. "Excellent! This chick's got it. I hope the rest of you gentlemen heard that. I want you to write that down and paste it to your bathroom mirror and recite it every day. That's your fuckin' mantra! Okay, we start filming Monday. Be here at six A.M. sharp!"

While everyone got up to leave, I sat in my chair, dazed, wondering how all this happened. Yes, I knew exactly that this show was going to be little more than a gay Jerry Springer with a lot of tight pants. Yes, I signed the contract to be on the show. Yes, I showed up today for the briefing. But as I sat there, I wondered why I had done this? For the fame? Probably not. My low self-confidence made me shun the limelight like a cockroach under a fluorescent kitchen light. For the money? Well, yeah. I had four condo rentals that weren't going to pay for themselves. And a mortgage on a money pit that I called home (or The Curse, depending on my mood that day). But still, I couldn't get the question out of my mind. Like a mass murderer at his arraignment, why did I do it? And the answer was that I didn't know.

Jeremy, sensing wrongly that I was starstruck, gave me a pep talk.

"You're going to be a star, baby. What's my little girl thinking about?"

I let the "little girl" pass as just another Hollywood-bullshit-make-small-talk. I looked him straight in the face. "I was thinking that being on this show was going to make spending a weekend with Liz and Dick Burton look like a Girl Scout Jamboree."

"That's the spirit," Jeremy exclaimed enthusiastically, clopping me hard on the back as I stood up to leave.

CHAPTER 5

I've Got A Funny Feeling About This

"So how was my movie star's first day?" Alex asked as I walked into our decoy office at the real-estate firm where we routinely gave too much of our commissions to our do-nothing brokerage. We mostly operated out of our home offices but used this one to store our huge files, make telephone calls, and more importantly, color copies.

"There's less tension at a Palestinian-Israeli summit meeting."

"The bitchiness has started already?"

"Oh, Alex, you have no idea. This show is going to descend into the depths of white trashiness."

"The guys look the part? One tooth in the front of their mouths to hook some fruit?"

"Alex, I didn't say these guys were from Desert Hot Springs. No, all the contestants are gorgeous models. Most are still working and one is in rehab."

"A model in rehab. I never thought I'd see the day," Alex said, insincerely shaking his head.

I took a stack of flyers for an overpriced home and dropped them all on the floor. "But behind the Estée Lauder eye rejuvenation creams and plastic Prada pants, their manners and breeding give 'em away. The weird thing is the French guy is the trashiest. Give him just one episode. He's going to strip the Kardashian family of their class. I always think of the French as being, well, you know, having taste."

"They adore Mickey Rourke."

"Okay, so there's a big, gaping hole in my theory. Gilles is nothing more than trash du traileur with a great body and face to match! And these guys are like what Gertrude Stein once said about Oakland, California."

"There isn't any there, there?"

"That's about the sum of it, Alex. They spend most of their time texting, or playing Angry Birds video games. The glitz is the substance."

"Amanda, they're models. What did you expect?"

"You'd think with all the time they've spent in London and Paris and Milan, some sophistication would rub off."

"I think the word you're looking for is not sophistication, but as you said, substance. Don't hold your breath. These kind of shows would turn Prince William into Snooki."

"Oh God, Alex, please don't mention *Jersey Shore*. I'm so afraid that Italy is never going to forgive us for letting those troglodytes film the show in Florence. Florence! Can you image it? The birthplace of the Renaissance! The city where all of Europe began to climb out of the Dark Ages, and the cast of *Jersey Shore* almost put it right back where it started in just a few weeks."

"Amanda, the guys on your show might not be Rhodes Scholars, but they could never descend that low. You know this is a reality show, Amanda. There's going to be bitchiness, cattiness, pettiness, and above all, manufactured drama. But do you think it's going to have good production values?"

"Good production values, Alex? This is one step up from a porn film."

"It's not that bad. At least Ian has good taste in his house."

"It's full of penises."

"It's full of male models, Amanda. What else could it be?"

"No, Alex. There are penises everywhere—sculptures, paintings, illustrations, pool floats."

"Oh, then Ian's not getting any."

I brightened up. "That's what I thought. Exactly." I sighed. "Well, Alex, there is a silver lining. Maybe."

"The paycheck?"

"No, that's expected."

"Possible future husbands?"

"No, that ain't gonna happen. I think I'm the only straight person on the show. Oh, wait a minute. Aurora Cleft... I think she's straight. I think."

"Aurora Cleft? What is she? British supermodel? Nazi she-wolf?"

"Both, but she's kinda short for the model thing. She's Ian's therapist, counselor, exorcist, whatever. But I like her. I think."

"She's the silver lining?"

"I'm going to make her my emotional airbag. A buffer, so to speak. All right, I'm going to hide behind her if I need to."

Alex gave me one of those stop-underestimating-yourself looks. "How about this: Why don't you work to stand out rather than hide in the shadows? I mean, that's what they hired you for."

"I'm there for the comic relief... to make others look good while they dance rings around me."

"Then don't let 'em do it. You're much smarter than

those vacuous models and musclehead pretty boys. Remember, the image you create on this show is going to stay with you for a long time."

"Like Janet Jackson's pierced and armored nipple at the Super Bowl? Great! I still can't get that image out of my head."

"I know, I still wake up screaming at night. That is one ugly boob . . . the veins, ugh! But back to the matter at hand. You're a smart aleck. You're funny. Why don't you put all those zingers you come up with to good use?"

"Oh, I don't know, Alex."

"Amanda, you said that these guys are vain, narcissistic, bitchy, and vacuous."

"Most of them are."

"So then it will be like shooting fish in a barrel. You're going to stand out if you play off these bad qualities. I mean, if these guys turn out to be as bad as you think they might be, they're not going to be likable. Ian is certainly not likable. Aurora seems like a hardass. You play it smart and witty, and you're going to steal the show since viewers are going to want someone to like. They'll identify with you because you'll be giving these guys the kick in the ass the viewers want them to get."

I got up to go, grabbing my briefcase.

"Where are you going?" Alex asked.

"To look through my shoe closet for a pair with really sharp toes. I'll call you later."

"Yes, Mrs. Gorky, I understand you're frustrated that your house hasn't sold yet and your neighbor's has. But as I told you, Lionel's house is 1,200 square feet larger, it has a drop-dead kitchen and new baths, and yours doesn't. Yours is kinda original. From 1957 . . . Yes, I know yours has the original Formica, and we described it as vintage in the brochures, but it's still gold-flecked Formica. . . . Yes, I understand that buyers are out for blood, but that doesn't change things. . . . Yes, I think they're bloodsuckers. . . . What? No, I wouldn't call them that . . . that's illegal. Listen, I understand . . . yes . . . I work in the market, I don't make it. No, I don't think it's a Jewish conspiracy. Well, I imagine that Lehman Brothers had some Jewish people working there, but . . . Yes, but I don't think that has anything to do with your house not selling. Let's give it a few more weeks, and let's talk about a price reduction at the end of the month. No, I think that's what we need . . . Yes, about $50,000. I'm sorry, Mrs. Gorky, I think that's what we need. Okay, I'll call you in a week. Okay, yes, I hear that. Fuckers, huh? Goodbye."

I hung up the phone like it weighed 300 pounds. I was back in the office with Alex after a short lunch.

"Is she still on the Jew-bastards rant?" Alex inquired.

"That was last week. Now she's after the Armenians."

"She's old Russia, isn't she? Probably missing the good ol' days of Stalin."

"Did you see the varicose veins in her legs that she tries covering up with the dark blue hose? And the naval pinafore dress and spectators! She looks like a casting call for the movie *Grey Gardens*. Alex, could you tell me why we took on this listing? I knew she was crazy the moment she walked into my open house two months ago."

"The lipstick?" he replied. "A telltale sign if there ever was one. Normal people can put theirs on and manage to hit most of their lips."

"I think she's better suited for living under a bridge instead of in a mid-century house. I don't know why we took this listing," I added exasperatedly.

"Money? Penance?"

"Alex, you forget that I'm Catholic. Life is penance."

"I never forget that you were raised Catholic because you remind me daily."

"That's because I suffer mental anguish from it every day of my life."

"That was almost thirty years ago. It's time to move on, Amanda."

"I can't. It's not just mental trauma. It's physical. Look at my hands. I still have ruler marks from when Sister Gerzaniks hit me because I colored Jesus's face black in second-grade Sunday school."

"Black?"

"The sister told us Jesus lived in the Middle East, where there are deserts and a lot of sun. So I figured Jesus would really be tan at the very least, and since someone had used all the burnt sienna crayons in the box, I used black."

"Sister Gerzaniks was a racist."

"She was. She pointed to a picture of Jesus, then a crucifix on the wall, and asked me if his face looked black to me."

"And what did you say?"

"I said that was just one artist's conception of what Jesus could have looked like."

"You did not. You couldn't have been more than eight."

"What could I say, Alex? She was towering over me and had the dreaded ruler in her hand. The one stained red from all the blood. Before I knew it, she brought it down on my hands. I'll never be a hand model again."

"Did you tell your mother about this? This is physical abuse."

"I did."

"And what did she say?"

"She said I probably deserved it. Real supportive."

"Did anyone tell Sister Gerzaniks that there is absolutely no description of Jesus in the Bible, so every painting or sculpture is completely manufactured. It all depends on the artist. It's not like we had a yearbook to look at."

"No one looks good in their high-school picture, Alex—except you. Imagine, Jesus with acne."

"The Holy pustule."

"We're supposed to be made in God's image, if you believe the Bible."

"Amanda, if there was a God, do you think he would run around looking like Paris Hilton?"

"So remind me again, Alex, why we have this listing? It's overpriced, the seller is psychotic, and no one is buying any homes."

Alex looked at me as if to say, y-e-s?

There it was, staring me in the face like an oversized sty. The Great Recession that was really a Depression, but nobody wanted to name it that because it was too scary. But you couldn't ignore it any more than you could a crack whore in your living room. It all started on Wall Street, with stock brokerages creating financial vehicles from borrowed overseas money with no wheels on them, lending money out to anyone who could successfully fog a mirror, to homeowners who bought houses at artificially inflated prices, then took out home equity loans with the false equity they had in their homes and spent it on masochistically ugly home improvements, more speculative housing buys, or boob jobs and cigarette boats capable of running down swimmers at over 100 miles an hour. It was a worldwide clusterfuck. It all was going along very nicely until the participants ran out of lube. Then things got uglier than an Amish fashion show.

Yes, we Realtors had our fine, manicured hands up to the third joints in this mess. We sold these overinflated houses by the thousands and made money like South American drug dealers. We lived like them too. Almost everyone was driving BMWs or Mercedes. The poorer agents drove Lexuses. All this wealth and fine living didn't go unnoticed either. Soon, everyone was getting into the business. Waitresses, school teachers, interior designers, followed by the just plain stupid and inept, while the corrupt brought up the rear. They exploded out of nowhere like a squeezed zit, bloating the ranks of agents while the State of California struggled to keep up with those applying. After all, all you had to do was have a car and a Department of Real Estate license. You didn't have to build a database of leads, follow up on them, do mailing, make phone calls, and build a business plan. And like Santa Claus, we all believed the lie, believing that home values were going to go up forever and ever. The rising tide was going to raise all boats, but ours was going to be a yacht. We were going to be stinking rich. And some of us were . . . for the life span of a fruit fly. Then the whole sorry mess began to collapse like a house of cards. Agents went bankrupt, walked away from their homes, drove those fancy cars off cliffs, or more dramatically, made their entire borrowed estate into a delicious bonfire. And there we stood, with sellers looking at us Realtors to bail their butts out of the sling.

The phone buzzed from the front desk.

"Yes, Gino?"

"Call for you from Jeff Stewart. He's on the warpath again."

"Great," I responded. "Put him through, Gino."

I looked at Alex for support. "Your turn to get shot," I commented, handing him the phone.

CHAPTER 6

Absence Makes the Heart Grow Fonder. Does That Apply to Sluts Too?

I went home that night after a fruitless afternoon. Ken, my detective with the Palm Springs police and my cautious and perpetual dating partner, had let himself in and was cooking.

"How was the first day of shooting?"

"Like a drive-by."

"That bad?"

"Actually, they didn't do any shooting today, just a get-to-know-your-enemy meeting. It's going to be a pit of snakes."

"Well, Amanda, sit down and I'll pour you a cucumber martini. That should make things right."

Into a frosted glass, he poured my favorite drink with care, then topped it off with a cucumber slice. Perfect. Like my ex, Alex.

"I've got some bad news for you, Amanda," he said, looking me straight in the eye.

"You're gay. I knew it! You dress too well. You're too handsome. You know how to cook. You have tasteful furniture in your condo."

"I'm not gay. I'm metrosexual."

I laughed like it was all a joke, when it really wasn't. After my first husband turned out to be gay, I've been waiting for the other Gucci shoe to drop with Ken. He's too much like a gay man to be straight. He assures me all the time. Fucks me until I'm crazy. And still I wonder. Once bitten, twice shy, I guess.

Ken continued, "No, I've got to leave town for a while. My mother fell."

"Oh, my God, is she all right?"

"She fell down the stairs into the basement. Didn't break a single bone, but she's pretty bruised up and in the hospital. I have to fly home and get her on her feet. I might be gone for a while."

"Of course, of course, Ken. Any idea how long this might take? A month?"

Ken shook his head.

"Two?"

Again, another sad shake. "Amanda, I really don't know. I have to get her on her feet again, make her house more accessible, and find someone to look in on her."

My face fell like a startled soufflé. "Well, okay. I'm sure I'll find something to do in the meantime. Maybe I'll take up snake handling. Or golfing. I need a hot, buff caddy following me around with a wood in his bag."

"It's only for a while, and you yourself said you wanted to take things slowly. This will give you some time off. Absence makes the heart grow fonder, they say."

"They also say that while the cat's away, the mice will play."

Ken looked surprised. "You?! Naw!"

"Well, you don't have to say it like I was made of pus. I do get other men who look at me from time to time."

"I wouldn't blame them."

"Mostly they're trying to figure out *what happened* to Kathleen Turner. Or they're gay and like my shoes. But I do get cruised by real straight men in this town. All two of them."

"I wouldn't be surprised. But for your information, not every man in Palm Springs is gay, you know. And don't worry, I'll come back eventually."

Just then, the weirdest thought flashed across my brain. Just for a nanosecond, but it was there nonetheless: I would be single while Ken was gone. I immediately dismissed the thought, but it left a vapor trail in my head that remained there for weeks. What frightened me was that here I get the partner I was so desperately looking for, and now I was being seduced by the notion of looking for someone else. Or at least stepping out to play. I hated dating. Hated it. But the fantasy of a naughty fling, well . . . This was followed by a wave of Catholic guilt that hit me like an Indonesian tsunami, yet I hadn't even done anything wrong . . . yet.

I continued in an attempt to hide my guilty feelings. "Well, I could use the time to work on my fudge sculpture."

"I didn't know you had an artistic side."

"Neither did I, but I've got to find something else to do besides hocking houses."

"I don't think real estate has been that bad for you. You've made some big money selling homes."

"Yeah, about three years ago."

"Where is it now?"

"Tied up in the several rental properties I have that are worth about half of what I paid for them. Or just plain pissed away."

"You pissed all that money away?"

"Well, like I said, I do have several rental properties. And a ton of nice shoes."

Ken shook his head, then smiled that smile, framed by those pillowy lips that made me fall for him—besides his husky-dog, ice-blue eyes and jet-black hair, graying ever so slightly at the temples.

"Amanda, the time will fly by. And before you know it, I'll be back in town."

"Sure," I replied, giving him a hug while my mind raced at the possibility of being on my own for a while. What was going on with me?

"Of course you should have fun while Ken is gone!" Regina replied incredulously.

I didn't want to lay my cards on the table with just anyone, but my secret was safe with Regina, my ageless neighbor. The old saying that there may be snow on the roof, but there's still a fire in the furnace below, fit Regina to a T. Occasionally, though, one of Regina's gentlemen callers merely left her with a burning sensation down below, if you know what I mean.

"You don't mean I should cheat on Ken, do you?" I asked.

"Amanda, Ken is a terrific guy. But you can't get all you want and need in one package."

"Yes, I can. Ken gives me support, he loves me, we have great sex. What more can a woman want?"

"Something different. Something exciting! The thrill that comes with sex with a complete stranger."

"Well, you've got something there," I admitted hesitantly. "Can I trust you with a thought I've been having lately?"

"Shoot."

"You know how I was so desperate to find a new partner after Alex and I divorced."

"Desperate wasn't the word for it. Pathetic would be a better fit."

"Oh, c'mon, Regina, I was lonely."

"That's why I encouraged you to get out and have some *funnnnnnnnn*."

"That's what would you call it, Regina?"

"Okay, extracurricular activities. Amanda, let me ask you another question. Are you and Ken going steady?"

"Steady? No, but he let me wear his varsity sweater."

"Funny. So what are the two of you to each other?"

"Regina, we were both in emotionally difficult breakups. We're just not rushing into anything. We're taking our time."

"And taking your time means the ability to explore others, since you're not tied down to each other."

I looked at Regina, wondering why she didn't go into trial law. "When you explain it like that, it doesn't sound like cheating at all. It sounds like personal fulfillment. Something that I not only deserve, but have a right to."

"Good, honey. Keep saying it to yourself like that over and over. Hey, I've got an idea. Let's go out tonight and have fun, just us two girls. We can head out to Aqua Bar."

"Regina, unless the crowd has changed since I was there last, the men there are mostly gay."

"Listen, sweetie, that hasn't stopped you or me before. Let's head out at nine."

CHAPTER 7

Girls Just Wanna Have Fun

Regina and I went out that very night. Ken had to pack, so he approved of us going out. Girls' night, he called it.

At nine, I sidled over to Regina's house just as she was emerging through the front door, locking it behind her.

"Get in," she instructed.

I knew she was going to drive, and that meant that we would take her car. Going out for a hot night on the town in a powder-blue, 1996 Oldsmobile Ninety-Eight wasn't exactly the kind of wheels you wanted to be seen in when trying to land hot guys, but Regina was Regina. What could you do but humor the situation?

I got in and slammed the door behind me. Good and solid. Like the door to a Spanish dungeon. Regina slid in, too, slammed the door, then had to slam it again since it wasn't shutting tight since "I sideswiped an olive tree outside Tropicana after happy hour last week."

For Regina, this meant one thing: She was a little too happy when she left the restaurant, er, bar. It wasn't the first time. She once hit a tree, and the only reason the cops managed to trace her car to the scene of the crime was that they followed the trail of car parts to her house. I decided I would be the designated driver on our way home later tonight.

She jammed the key into the ignition and let the car beep incessantly, adjusted the rearview mirror to make a last-minute check of her makeup, turned the mirror back into a more useful position, started the car, and Lady Gaga's "Bad Romance" exploded from the speakers, scaring the bejesus out of me in the process. Obviously, Regina was out last night and forgot to turn the volume down. I know. I heard her pull in at 2:30 last night.

She clapped her hands like a mad scientist.

"So what's on the menu tonight?" she asked, throwing the car into reverse and steering the land leviathan down the driveway. I watched her mailbox pass a mere three inches from my window, but at least she missed it. "How about Aqua? The night has cooled down. I think a drink outside would be just perfect tonight."

Because Palm Springs is surrounded by towering mountains and is, well, a desert, the nights in October can be quite pleasant. So, as a result, many of the bars in town are outside. Or most of them have an inside and an outside component. Aqua had a huge outdoor bar. In fact, almost all of Aqua was outside.

As Regina crossed Alejo Road and steered the Queen Mary down Palm Canyon Drive, I realized that although I've lived next to Regina for a few years, I've never been out on the town with her. I've gone to dinner, parties, fundraisers, the movies, and numerous gay bars. But never out looking for straight men.

Regina made a right into the parking lot next to Aqua, slowed to a crawl as she scanned the crowd outside at the bar, then drove on.

"No cute guys in there tonight. Plus, the crowd is a little thin," she commented. She was the Zagat guide to dating in Palm Springs.

I was amazed. "Regina, you just saved me hours of time wasted sitting in a bar waiting to meet someone. I would have gone inside, sat there for several drinks, and left completely deflated an hour later. You just summed up the place in five seconds and moved on."

"Amanda, honey, I've been going to bars a lot longer than you have. You have to know how to work them so you don't waste time . . . and when you're my age, you don't have a lot of time to waste."

We drove by several bars until we settled on Mercury. Safely inside, I felt the need to pry Regina's barhopping secrets from her.

"First off, Amanda, check out the parking lot. An empty lot means a slow night. Certain bars are always good: Mercury, Tropicana, Chi-Chi's, and Drink Here Now. But remember, certain nights are better than others. Sit at the bar, but avoid bars that you can't walk around completely . . . you don't want to get stuck in a cul-de-sac at the end of a bar. Most men will turn around, figuring the fishing's no good at the end of the bay. Choose bars with good bartenders, and I don't mean those who pour without a spout. You want to sit at the bar where the bartender will chat you up when things are slow. A good one will know that and keep you entertained if you don't have a good prospect at that moment. Also, a good bartender will clue you in if a patron is horny or lonely. Enough about me. So how's the show shaping up?"

"Okay, I guess."

"What do you mean *okay*? Honey, you should be excited. Surrounded by gorgeous men."

"Regina, they're gay. I'm just the token fag hag."

"That's why you're on the show? As a beard?"

"These guys don't need beards, Regina. They're so out, you could spot them from the Space Station."

"So what's the deal with the hesitation? Stage fright?"

"A little."

"So spill it. What's holding you back from having a good time on the show . . . and making some big money?"

"I wouldn't be counting on big money. It's good, though."

"Spill."

"I don't know, Regina. It's not the fact that I'm going to be on TV. It's . . . it's . . ."

"Yes . . . ?"

"I have a bad feeling about it—the show. Right here," I said, pointing to my gut.

"I had that too. Turned out to be cramps."

"Regina, there's a lot of money at stake. Millions! And I get the feeling that these guys could be ruthless."

"I would be ruthless for those sums. You expect foul play could raise its coiffed head?"

"I would plan on it."

"So what are you thinking, Amanda? Sabotaged wardrobes? Preparation H substituted for facial creams?"

"No, murder."

"Shit!" Regina exclaimed. "One contestant eliminating the other?"

"I know it sounds crazy, but yes."

"But that would end the show and maybe the contest."

"Regina, you haven't met the producer. He wants ratings, and he's the type to stop at nothing to get them."

"You mean he might murder one of the contestants just to get viewers?"

"I never thought of it that way, Regina. I was just thinking of one contestant eliminating another."

"There's another possibility you haven't considered, Amanda."

"And what's that?"

"Someone murdering Ian."

"But that would be killing the goose that laid the golden egg. It makes no sense, Regina."

"Yes, it does, Amanda. It does if someone wants to stop Ian from laying the egg in the first place."

"Wait a minute. I'm confused with your avian analogy."

"My what?"

"Your bird theory."

"What?"

"Skip it. So what did you mean, Regina?"

"That someone would have every reason to bump Ian off before he gives away all that money to some dumb model. This person would want to keep the line of succession just the way it is now."

"How many mystery novels have been based on that premise, Regina?"

"About a million. You better watch out, honey, or you might find yourself in the middle of one. Let's have another drink."

I had two drinks; Regina had a few more than that. She introduced me to a handful of people, but for the most part, this night was just like all the others when I went looking for a man. I met a few, chatted with a few, and went home empty-handed. Not that I was planning on bringing anyone home so soon. The point was, my life hadn't really changed: No one really paid much attention to me.

We made it home safely that night with me behind the wheel, and after I bid Regina good night, I went promptly to bed. The next morning, I got up and prepared for the day, but I couldn't get Regina's thoughts out of my head—nothing you want running around in your head when you're about to be on television for the first time. How far might someone go to secure a vast fortune? The answer that resounded in my head was simple . . . and frightening: pretty damn far.

CHAPTER 8

I'm Ready for My Close-Up, Mr. DeMille

It was the first day of shooting. We were starting early, but I had to make a stop before I drove over to Ian's house. I had to check on one of my rentals since the tenants had stopped paying rent and I wanted to make sure they had moved out as promised. I could have had them evicted, but that takes a long time and a lot of money, so I talked them into leaving peacefully and, in return, I wouldn't report them to a credit agency.

When the money was really rolling in until the economic Big Bang, I bought several condos that I figured I could rent out for a few years, then sell at a big profit since everything was going to go up forever and ever. This one was in a development in central Palm Springs, modern with a two-story atrium, and really very dramatic, inside and out. I fell in love with it the day I bought it.

When I walked up the sidewalk to the front door, something was amiss with the front door: it was a-missing. As I walked inside, I quickly discovered that everything else was missing, too—the stove, microwave, refrigerator, bathroom vanities, even the toilets. Yes, the toilets. Did they take them dirty? Needless to say, I wasn't in a good mood when I left the condo and headed over to Ian's house.

As I pulled up to Ian's house, it looked more like a bee-hive than a place where an over-pampered multimillionaire hairdresser lived. There were half a dozen trucks parked on the street, with men carrying equipment, and women bran-dishing walkie-talkies—money was being spent on a grand scale.

I was stopped by a frantic woman with a walkie-talkie who, after ascertaining that I was a member of the show and not a crazed lunatic trying to crash the shoot, waved me into the parking area outside Ian's garage. Once again, my Toyota Land Cruiser was the shabbiest car in the lot, showed up by the Bentleys, Mercedes-Benz SLS, and, landing at the top of the car heap, a beige, two-toned May-bach Landaulet—Ian's, with the vanity license plate spell-ing WHAT IF.

I was directed to a tent that had been set up for wardrobe and makeup, which I thought was odd, since this was sup-posed to be a reality show. Apparently, they didn't want *too* much reality. I brought my own bathing suit, opening cred-its outfit, and several changes of clothing, all of which were put aside in a closet by my stylist, Jacob. Pronounced Yak-obb, even though he didn't have an accent.

"First thing, we're going to shoot the opening credits, where you appear with your name. Jeremy wants you look-ing fabulous, since this shot will not only open each show, but they'll use this shot in the promos too," Jacob said, turning me around slowly and sizing me up like a cut of yellowfin tuna at a Japanese fish auction.

"Promos?"

"The commercials they run to advertise the show. Also

on the Web site, blogs, etcetera, etcetera. You're gonna be all over the world. For your credit shot, Jeremy wanted you in this little number," he said. "The color is more color-friendly to the cameras than the stuff you brought."

Little is right: There was very little to it. It looked like at one time it was a legitimate dress, but that it had been clawed by a cougar. Folded up, I imagined it filled a measuring cup with room to spare.

"It's awfully sheer," I mentioned, a fact that fell on deaf ears.

"Let's see you in that first, then we'll do your hair," he said, shushing me off to a curtained booth to change.

I slipped into the dress, and yes, it was awfully sheer. Thank goddess I worked out, rode eighty miles a week on my road bike, and hiked every other week. When I presented myself to Jacob and looked at myself in the mirror, I could see what was wrong with it right away. My nipples were plainly visible.

"Jacob?" I suggested. "You might want to tape over my nipples . . . they're showing. We don't want that on national television, do we?"

I received a withering look that would have killed a cactus.

"Why do you think Jeremy picked out the dress? He wants viewers to see your nipples."

Clearly, I wasn't getting through to Jacob. "I'm not sure that's such a good idea."

"Trust me, sweetie, we'll make it look tasteful. We're not gonna make you look like a street walker."

As soon as Jacob had uttered those words, they lodged in my head like buckshot from Dick Cheney's gun. I was going to look like a slut on national television.

"It looks great. Now don't worry, Miranda."

"Amanda."

"Yeah, whatever. Look, you're in my hands; my job is to make you look great for the show. C'mon. This is a gay show, not *The Real Housewives of Orange County*. Now there's a truckload of skanky pole dancers for you. Trust me . . . pleeeeaaassseee?"

"Okay, Jacob. I'm going to trust you."

"Great, you're going to look fabulous! Let's see the hair stylist now."

"Stylist? I think my hair looks great now."

This time, a look of *do-you-really-think-that-you-poor-thing?*

"Jacob, I have a hair stylist here in town. Roberto. Yes, he's a little dramatic, but he does a good job and he's good with color. I mean, yes, he does like driving down to Oceanside to pick up Marines occasionally, but . . ."

Jacob stopped leading me toward the hair and makeup styling tent, turned around, then put his hand over my mouth.

"Are you through?"

"Yes, I guess so. I'm just a little nervous."

"That's normal. Being on television for the first time."

"No, not that. I do have a guy who styles my hair here in town. If I get it styled for the show, Roberto is going to know next time I see him."

"He'll get over it."

"He's a dramatic Brazilian queen. You don't want to piss off a hairdresser, especially him, any more than you want to aggravate a plastic surgeon as you go under the knife or an airplane pilot before takeoff. They can make life really ugly for you if they want."

"Amanda, darling, who is this whole show about?"

"Ian Forbes."

"That's right. The man who made millions cutting hair correctly. Do you think Jeremy is going to let just anyone cut hair on this show? He knows Ian is going to be watching everything. So relax and trust me. You're going to have Sebastian from Ian's own salon in Beverly Hills do your hair. He's refused to style some of the biggest names in Hollywood, he's that good. "

"Shit. Sorry. I guess I am lucky."

"You don't know how lucky you are. You are going to look so great, your life is never going to be the same again."

Little did I know how right he was going to be.

I got my hair styled and I had to agree, in the hands of a talented stylist, a lump of clay could be made into a masterpiece. In fact, it was a revelation that made me deliriously happy, then angry for all the years and thousands of dollars I'd spent thinking I couldn't improve my appearance any more than what the gods gave me. My problem is that I was hiring amateurs. I looked in the mirror as Sebastian finished up on me and I looked at my reflection—it struck me that I wasn't a bad-looking woman. Or, at least now I wasn't. The reality was that there was always great potential there. It just took someone like Sebastian to give me enough style to make me shine.

"There," Sebastian said, giving me a hand mirror so I could admire myself up close. "You look like Jane Lynch from *Glee*. Sexy, smart, not too polished. Natural. Plus, it helps play up your nose."

"My nose?" I asked like a bleary-eyed child. "Play it up?"

"Oh, yes. I like your nose. Very come-fuck-me."

I never thought about a nose inviting fornication, but I suppose it was possible. Over the years, I've heard of guys getting turned on by everything from writhing in custard to wearing certain wristwatches. Yes, wristwatches. The right kind of wristwatch can make some guys cum. Go figure.

"Come . . . ?"

"Your nose. It is very sexy. Very virile, aristocratic."

I put my hand on Sebastian's arm. "You find my nose aristocratic? When I think of aristocratic noses, I think of pointy, sharp ones like the British."

"Well, then, Amanda, you haven't spent enough time in Europe. The continent. The French. The Italians. Germans. All big. You are beautiful, now go and make love to the camera."

As I was escorted away by Jacob, I had to ask the question: "Is Sebastian straight?"

"Yes, he is. His girlfriend is absolutely stunning," Jacob added.

"Does she have a big nose?"

Jacob thought for a moment. "I don't really remember. But he seemed to like you."

"Nooooo, Jacob! He was just being nice."

"No, I've seen him style lots of women. He doesn't flirt with them like he did with you."

I thought no more about what Jacob said for the time being. I got into my dress and when I was squeezed into it, they made me up. I stole another look in the mirror and, Jesus, if I didn't look fantastic. It was a whole new way of thinking for me.

I got to the set and they were just finishing up shooting Keith MacGregor. Keith was attired in a black silky shirt unbuttoned practically to his waist, showing off his hairless chest and tan. And, if I wasn't mistaken, his padded crotch. Now, I'm no slut, but I have seen a number of male boxes in my time, and I can tell when one is not all-natural. Keith's crotch wasn't anything to sneeze at, but it seemed more than prominent, compliments of the stylist staff. I wonder if they were serving kielbasa at the lunch. I mean, it ran a few inches down his right leg.

As for the rest of him, Keith had that relaxed, easygoing presence in front of the camera and acted like he spent all his life in front of one. He probably did just one take, just like Elizabeth Taylor.

My television debut was a little different. I didn't even have to talk. All I had to do was smile and turn toward the camera with my body. But I couldn't get it right. Take after take, and I couldn't act natural. Go figure . . . a reality show and I couldn't be real.

The assistant director, Matthew, finally spoke up, "Amanda, just stop trying to be a character. Be yourself."

"Easy for you to say," I replied. "I'm still trying to figure out that one."

Eventually, the cameraman either got the promo footage he wanted or he just plain gave up. He released me to get into my own personal swimsuit, which apparently wasn't so hideous, so I was allowed to head out to the pool area. In hindsight, I should have turned back right then and there. But that's the problem with hindsight. It only comes to you after you really need it.

CHAPTER 9

Open Mouth, Insert Prada Loafer

As I saw the pool area, I almost gasped. It was beyond spectacular. The huge pots of cactuses that ringed the pool were retrofitted with blooming flowers that would burn up after a single day of shooting. Fabric cabanas lined the south end of the pool, and even though the day was pleasantly warm, misting systems spewed clouds of evaporative water, providing a cool oasis through the miracle of pressured water and the laws of thermodynamics. There were buff waiters wearing skintight neoprene short shorts that clung to every crack and bulge. On each tray of food that the waiters carried were incredibly elaborate finger foods and appetizers that trumpeted hours and hours of cooking and hand assemblage. And then there was the alcohol. It poured from bottles that seemed to be everywhere. Everywhere. This was reality?

As a tray of bubbling champagne flutes with the label of Dom Perignon prominently displayed for the cameras floated by, I grabbed a glass and downed it, bolstering my courage.

When everyone was in place, I felt like the science nerd

at a party of high-school cheerleaders. So I did what any socially outcast person would do: I moved nearest people who were the least threat to me, and that person turned out to be Aurora. We camped out in one of the cabanas, owing to Aurora's third bout with skin cancer.

It was then that a cameraman moved in on the two of us. There was no hiding.

The assistant, who was part of the audio dialogue, prompted us to start the ball a rollin'.

The question: You've met the contestants. So how do you think they're going to fare?

Like a coward, I turned the question over to Aurora, who immediately slipped into her persona, which was a natural. She looked at, no, confronted, the camera, then gave her verdict: "I think they all have a good shot at winning Ian's hand, seeing that we've just started. But I have my eyes on Gilles. He's rude, arrogant, and self-absorbed. I don't know if he's going to make it."

I would have thought that these qualities would make him the perfect match for Ian. In all candor, these were the qualities that pushed Ian to the top of the international world of beauty. He was not only known for styling some of the world's most famous women, but he gained his real fame by berating those same women for seeing shitty hair stylists. His famed disagreement with Elizabeth Taylor over a hairstyle reduced her to tears. It also made him a star. And even more famous. And infinitely desirable.

The camera swung to me, waiting for me to add something wonderful and remarkable. I froze up. I knew I was supposed to add something to what Aurora had so adroitly thrown out there, but I was so nervous I couldn't come up with a great, insightful sound bite. Nothing. So I merely said what popped into my head: "I don't know what Gilles is after, but he seems like gold-digging Eurotrash."

After it was out of my mouth, I realized that I should have been more diplomatic, but goddammit, this show was after reality and that's the reality that the champagne fed me. Fuck 'em.

Aurora tried valiantly to cover up the mess I had made, then sat in.

"I think what Amanda is trying to say is that Gilles has preconceived ideas of his worth as Ian's possible partner and heir, and they don't necessarily coincide with what's good for Ian. As for the rest of the guys, what I saw on my first meeting appalled me. Most of the men were texting, playing video games, and not paying attention to information about this program," she said, jabbing her pointy index-finger talon toward the ground for emphasis. "You'd think that they would be taking this whole situation a lot more seriously! I mean, if I were in the position to potentially inherit the kind of money that would make me secure for life and have a famous lover to boot, I would throw myself into the effort. But these guys are used to putting on some fancy clothes in Paris or New York and walking down a runway and having people fawn over them. Well, that's not going to happen here. If these guys think they're going to flash some white teeth, wear tight trousers, flirt with Ian, and be declared the best match for him, they better think again. We will have to see how things turn out. I don't have *any* favorites yet, but today will produce some winners"— she flipped her head to camera number two for emphasis— "and some *real* losers."

Okay, so her response was a tad better than mine. My first episode and I had blown it. To top it off, I had blurted

79

out my bombshell while I was drunk. No, make that tipsy. That was my official story and I was going to stick to it. The sad thing is that what I had said was what I felt about Gilles. My reality. He really was a piece of gold-digging Eurotrash. What Ian saw in such people mystified me, but I guess a pretty face, washboard abs, and huge uncut dick added up to qualities that an over-the-hill, overweight hair stylist nearing sixty-seven would leap for. For me, it seemed ludicrous that the majority of the human race leaped toward those who provided a great face or a hot bod. And as we got older, you would think that we would be past the shell game of good looks, but as we got older and more able to afford the young, desperate people jumped at youth. The saying that "Old age and treachery always win over youth and skill" seemed like a lie perpetrated by ugly old queens. I can't tell you how many times I've been dining in local restaurants or perusing the local modern furniture stores only to see a January-December romance. The young escort leading the old queen around by the ring in his nose, buying $35,000 sofas, $140,000 cars, and Viagra by the barrel. The face and body always won. But not while I was still alive. Not on my watch. Not this time.

The cameramen moved on since it appeared that Aurora and I were done. They concentrated on Ian, who was holding court like King Louis XIV, his courtiers sitting in rapt attention to a story of how he threw Sharon Stone out of his salon one day when she requested that he weave bits of bark and leaves into her hair for an awards show. (She was trying to get in touch with nature.)

And that was that. Until lunch, that is. We were all herded to the canteen tents, where the only food being served was devoid of carbs. Just meat and steamed vegetables. Jeremy had seen to it that no one on the show developed unsightly bulges while the season was being filmed. This was a reality show and reality was thin.

As I sat across from Aurora, who went on and on about her impressions about the contestants and how she saw their chances (after basically one meeting), I noticed some of the weirdest eating habits I had ever laid eyes on. Aleksei was drinking his Diet Coke through a straw. That might not sound weird, but he stuck the straw a good six inches down his throat, then like a snake, sucked up the caramel-colored liquid and swallowed it in waves, like a snake trying to ingest a raccoon. I pointed out this strange phenomenon to Aurora, who dismissed it with an I've-seen-it-all wave of her black-fingernail–tipped hand.

"Eating disorder?" I offered.

"Teeth bleaching. He doesn't want to get them stained."

"But why would that matter? Apparently they aren't ever supposed to smile, have a thought, or eat as part of their job."

"Oh, there's nothing these guys won't do to remain perfect. Most of them suffer from body dysmorphia."

"And that's a mortal fear of getting your teeth stained?"

"It's an obsession with perceived defects in a person's body."

"In whose body?"

"The body of the sufferer."

"Oh, I thought it might involve finding defects in another person's body."

"That's another disorder, Amanda."

"And that is called . . . ?"

"Bitchiness. No, these guys can't stop obsessing with the idea that specific parts of their bodies are imperfect. They keep me and a lot of plastic surgeons in business."

"Well, Aurora, I guess that accounts for all the plastic surgeons we have in southern California."

"Amanda, it's not just the surgeons. There are hoards of people willing to do anything to indulge the crazy ideas these guys have. There's someone to pluck your eyebrows, suck the fat out of your abdomen, put weights on your balls to make them hang lower, and even people who will bleach your asshole. One to two percent of the world suffers from it," Aurora reported, a pride emanating from her grasp of the facts.

"I don't believe it."

"No, it's true. About two in every hundred."

"No, not the dysmorphia statistics, Aurora. The . . . the . . . er . . . anal bleaching."

"Getting rid of the chocolate starfish?" she replied naughtily.

"So they get their . . . this area dyed because . . . ?"

"Two reasons. One, aesthetics. Two, it makes them look younger. The way they see it, a whiter asshole says it hasn't been—how do I say this—tinted with time. White teeth, white asshole."

"Two phrases I never want to hear again in the same sentence. But what does this have to do with modeling? With the possible exception of Thierry Mugler, I don't think any designer would ask these guys to expose their assholes on the catwalk."

"You don't understand body dysmorphia, Amanda. Like most dysfunctions, they're perceived. Their existence is in the eye of the beholder. These guys spend hours poring over their bodies, waxing, tweezing, and trimming. They examine every part of their bodies . . . even the parts most of us don't see. But *they* see them—the flaws. And they strive for a perfection they can't ever reach, because time is either keeping one step ahead of them, or their perceptions change, so what was considered perfect last week needs changing, plucking this week. It never ends."

"And all this attention to appearance is why these guys look so good?"

"That, and good genes," Aurora replied, scanning the guys around the pool.

"I know, you can spout all the bullshit you want about societal values, aesthetics, blah blah blah, but there is something about these guys that makes you look at them. Even when they're not made up, they stand out."

"Scientists think it has to do with pleasing proportions and exceptional symmetry. I don't know what it is either, Amanda. They do look abnormally handsome, don't they?"

I sighed. "They have such a leg up in life with their looks. I must have spent seven thousand dollars in my lifetime on rejuvenation creams and all I'm doing is reanimating the dead."

"Don't get all depressed now, Amanda. But there's a lot underneath the beauty that isn't pretty. These guys also suffer because of their looks: visual perfectionism. They won't even go out and get the mail without looking perfect. Look at David Laurant. He has a different, expensive look every single day. One day the hair is white and flipped up, the next it's pasted down and lying flat. Three days from now it will be dyed black. Obsession with image."

"Aurora, you know all this from just observation?"

"Oh, I know David is obsessed with his image. Gilles is

so narcissistic that his therapy should consist of nothing more than staring into a small hand mirror with the words '*You Are Beautiful and Perfect*' printed on the surface. Gilles is also incapable of feeling empathy toward any human being. Keith has fears of abandonment and sexual dysfunction that sometimes cripple him. Marcus Blade is another body dysmorphic, taking so many steroids that he almost blew out several arteries a year ago. Drake has a deep-seated need to exert power over men sexually. And Ian . . . Ian. Don't get me started. He's self-obsessed, narcissistic, vain, and uses his money and power to control everyone around him, both through sexual and financial means."

"Aurora, I'm not sure you should be telling me all this. What happened to doctor–patient confidentiality?"

Aurora gave a quick laugh. "Amanda, the patients I usually work with are important, successful people. You're unlikely to associate with them."

"Not them, Aurora," I replied, knocking her off the pedestal I had previously placed her on. "I mean the guys here on the show. What you're telling me is highly confidential."

"Oh, I don't treat these guys here. Just Ian. The psychiatrists who work with all the other guys told me all this."

Just then, the three large-screen televisions scattered around the lunch area sprung to life with footage of Keith MacGregor talking to Aleksei while they casually stood around in bathing suits that covered about as much as a playing card. We were then treated to various scenes of the individual contestants capturing their trepidations about being able to win the contest and why they were going to be declared Ian's heir—in equal portions. The editors threw in footage of Aurora, the consummate actor, delivering lines to the cameras like she had grown up cutting her baby teeth on a telephoto lens.

What struck me about what had been captured already on film was how the cameramen seemed to call all the shots for the show and managed to create a show just from their roving cameras. With just a little push, the show seemed to roll along on its own.

Then, up came the part where I called Gilles gold-digging Eurotrash. I heard gasps from a few of the guys, but when I shot a glance over toward Jeremy, he was smiling from ear to ear, Medea smiling over the deaths of her children.

Gilles, who was sitting out in front of me, didn't turn around. But I could see him slowly, almost imperceptibly shake his head from side to side as if he couldn't believe what he had just heard. And to tell the truth, neither could I. It was like another person had said what I had just blurted out. While the rest of the footage flashed by, no one seemed to care from that point on. After all, the fart had been let into the room and it wasn't clearing anytime soon.

After probably looking up the words gold digging on Wikipedia, Gilles was out for blood on the afternoon shoots. Aurora and the cameramen, sensing that this was going to be an explosive issue, followed me like a cat on the trail of an overturned fish truck.

As usual, I clung to Aurora for sustenance. We sat on the expensive chaise lounges around the pool, nibbling on outrageously expensive Japanese sushi finger foods, waiting for the cameramen to arrive, presumably to capture Gilles plunging an escargot fork into my heart. It was weird not knowing what was occurring elsewhere in the show. Occasionally, we overlapped and saw what was happening in other parts of the filming, but it never added up to a whole. It was like a magic show, where you were shown the ace of spades and expected to construct the rest of the magic trick, backward. At any one time, you had only part of the equation. The editors, bless their union-bound hearts, would take the twos, fives, and queens and kings and make it into a straight flush, a coherent program.

So, as I felt safe and secure with Aurora, my protectorate, Gilles stormed up to me and confronted me like an ancestral harpy. I stood up to meet him.

"Zo, you zink I ham a gold-digging U-O-trash? Let us zee how much of you izz real," he said, pulling my swimsuit top down in front of the rolling cameras.

What I did next was true reality. No scripting. I slapped him so hard across the face, his diamond stud earring flew off and into the pool, a good fifteen feet away. I'm not kidding. I actually watched it fly through the air in a perfect arc and land in the pool with a tiny plink. Even better, as I looked back at Gilles, I could still see my handprint clearly on his face, the fingers clearly and painfully outlined across his perfect skin.

You could have heard an ant sneeze.

I have never been a violent person, but it was so weird. It was like I had no other choice than to do what welled up in me like a volcanic explosion. And it felt good. Someone had done me wrong. No, violated me. And I struck back with total justification. Okay, I only did what everyone who probably ever came in contact with Gilles wanted to do within seconds of meeting him, but the point was, I did it. And it made me feel powerful. Really powerful.

As I stood there pulsing with adrenaline, Gilles seemed to freeze. I do believe it was the first time anyone had ever

A NOT SO MODEL HOME

stood up to him, especially a woman. He held his Gallic nose high in the air in defiance, both of us unwilling to back down. While there was still noise from all the other groups at the pool party, everyone in our little circle stood motionless, breathless. Then, Gilles blinked and turned haughtily away, dismissing me with a downward wave of his hand, the cameras trailing him like a pack of hyenas following a lion with fresh kill still in his mouth. I had won.

Aurora, waiting for the drama to pass—and to let the cameras get a reaction shot of her—raised her wineglass silently in a toast to me with a silent nod of acceptance. No, admiration. One tough bitch to another . . . in a gay man's world. When word spread throughout the pool party that I had "bitch-slapped the bitch," other members of the cast came to either shake my hand or just stare at me.

It was the start of my short, meteoric climb in notoriety. One that I barely began to perceive. But one that was going to produce changes in my life that I could not see at the moment. Yet, I did feel at one with myself for the time being. It was refreshing.

Of course, The Slap, as it came to be known, was just what Jeremy and his cameramen were looking for. I think it was at this point that I realized what a pivotal role the cameramen played. Despite my reservations that any portion of this show was going to have a plethora of reality, it was the cameramen who knew what would look good on TV, and they knew how to get it. Since the segment television producer wasn't always around to narrate off camera, the cameramen often prompted the contestants to make a statement or offer an opinion on what just happened. And since I had effectively stolen the first show single-handedly with my slap, the cameramen were corralling the men into making response segments to sprinkle in after the actual event had occurred. I overheard the responses for the most part, since the guys weren't sitting that far away. Strangely, the men were all pretty much supportive, but their dramatic reactions consisting of popped eyes and a few whistles intended to upstage me failed miserably. Aleksei commented that seeing a woman's naked body—or any part of it—made him want to puke. The first show belonged to me, hands down. But the genie was out of the bottle. In one single day, the men went from consummate models to being consummate actors.

And that was pretty much all for the taping of the first show of *Things Are a Bit Iffy*. The cast was jazzed up, Gilles was pissed off, Jeremy was beside himself—everyone was happy. Except me.

CHAPTER 10

The Slap Heard 'Round the World

That night, I went over to Alex's place. As he was pouring a cucumber martini for the both of us, Alex asked me how the filming went. I told him that there had been a kerfuffle.

"A kerfuffle? Did you just become a Tudor?"

"Well, I kinda slapped Gilles."

"Kinda slapped?"

"Okay, I bitch-slapped him."

"Whyyyyy?"

"Because he pulled down the top of my swimsuit and exposed my breasts."

"I thought this was a gay show, not an episode of *Girls Gone Wild.*"

"It *is* a gay show. I'm the token fag hag."

Alex was trying to figure out things. "So why would an obnoxious, gay French male model pull down the top of your swimsuit?"

"Ah, well, that's just the way he is," I said, lying through my newly whitened teeth. (So what if I wanted my teeth to look good for TV. I recently had them bleached . . . so sue me.)

"Amanda . . ." Alex started. "I can tell when you're lying."

"How so?"

"You don't look me in the eye and you start fiddling with something with your hands . . . like you're fiddling with my salt shaker. So spill it."

"I called him money-grubbing Eurotrash or something like that."

"No argument there from what you've told me about him, but I suppose you did this in front of a camera?"

"Pretty much. Yup."

"You had too much champagne, didn't you?"

"Now, why would you jump to that conclusion, Alex?"

"Amanda, we may have been married for only five years, but I know you very well. Your mouth runs free when you've had too much champagne."

"I blame it on the bubbles."

"So, are they going to put that segment on the show?"

"Oh, I don't think so, Alex," I said, lying through my pearly whites again, but mostly lying to myself.

"I'd check YouTube as soon as you can. I'll bet they've uploaded that scene already."

"Alex, they just filmed us this afternoon. It's eight o'clock right now. They wouldn't have had enough time to get it on there already. You're just getting way out ahead of yourself."

"Oh yeah, let's see," Alex said, clapping his hands in anticipation as he flipped the lid open on his MacBook Air and the computer screen leapt to life. He typed in some search topics, scrolled through a list of videos, then spun the laptop around for me to see. And there it was. The title? "Things Are a Bit Iffy: The Bitch Slap." I had to admit it, the title wasn't especially catchy, but it was optimized for search engine results. Meaning? It was probably going to go viral. Unfortunately.

I looked at the still frame from the video, afraid to click on the movie and watch myself broadcast to the entire world. My hand trembled as I clicked on the mouse and the movie began to play. Alex pulled in closer to get a good look.

After the intro that set up the premise of the show, what I saw was me saying that Gilles seemed "like gold-digging Eurotrash." This was followed by several reaction shots that were clearly taken long after the slap but edited in as if they had occurred immediately after it to make everything seem like it had all taken place in real time. I watched in horror as the clip led up to Gilles confronting me. I realized what would happen next and, unfortunately, I was not disappointed. The video showed Gilles pulling down my swimsuit top to expose my breasts, which were pixilated, only to the point of passing the censors. It was clear to every man, woman, child, and pervert that I had nothing to be embarrassed about in the endowment department.

It was the second loudest laughter I had ever heard out of Alex in all the years I had known him. The first, in case you're interested, was when we were alpine hiking and we stopped for a rest and Alex went to pee. I took the occasion to let out a fart just as Alex returned and I turned around to see a party of eight hikers resting silently above me on an overhanging rock. So now you know.

I was mortified. I would never be able to go out again, work again, even shop for groceries again. And it had all happened in less than five seconds. I couldn't believe that it was me I was looking at. I had gone from a successful Realtor to a piece of white trash showing her tits. It was surreal . . . just surreal.

I scrolled down a few more videos only to find that a dozen or so YouTube contributors had already downloaded the scene and re-edited it to create comical versions. One was entitled "Great Bitch Slaps of History," where the editor had pieced together some of the most renowned slaps in film history. My fifteen seconds of fame was rated higher than *Vivacious Lady*, with seven, count 'em, seven slaps, *Airplane, In the Heat of the Night*, and *The Godfather*. But no matter how good my slap was, probably chocking up points because mine was not a scripted one, the viewer who posted the film felt I just couldn't compete with Faye Dunaway's famous camp slap in *Mommie Dearest*. I had to concede defeat: How could you compete with Joan?

This video post was followed by another compilation of famous movie slaps—and mine—scored to the tune of Pat Benatar's "Hit Me with Your Best Shot." Clever. This was followed by a motley assortment of not-funny re-edits that usually had characters wearing bad wigs and trying pathetically to re-enact my glorious moment on the screen in basement rec rooms in New Jersey. I mean, we're talking hours since I pulled my slap. Hours! Alex got a great laugh out of all of them, especially the really unfunny videos, but what really struck me was how quickly this stuff got spread all across the Internet. It was like Facebook and Twitter photos of Congressmen in skimpy, tight athletic shorts showing obvious cock lines; they spread faster than pictures of Paris Hilton's beaver. The number of views said it all: In the short time my slap had been posted by the public relations people at Q Channel, some of the videos had had over 5,000 views. And climbing. What I forgot was how much time some people spend on the Internet, endlessly cruising for the funny, the weird, and the downright embarrassing.

During dinner, Alex told me to forget the whole thing, but I kept running over and over the same thought in my head: I will never get over this, never. Even after I went home that night to my perennially unfinished house in a state of perpetual remodeling and was greeted by Knucklehead, my rescued Labradoodle who erupted in a chorus of gleeful barking, the same words kept repeating in my head: *You're a Kardashian now.*

CHAPTER 11

Being World Famous For Fifteen Minutes Is Far Too Long

I got up early the next morning, and like a criminal returning to the scene of the crime, I started up my iMac and poured some coffee. I came back to my computer as it loaded my home page on Yahoo. I sped through the day's headlines, and at the bottom, what I saw almost made me fall off my chair. The last headline: SLAPPING VIDEO GOES VIRAL. I clicked on the link to see that "Great Bitch Slaps of History" had climbed from about 7,000 views last night to over 420,000. The other videos had jumped as well, but "Great Bitch Slaps" was chewing up the bandwidth. I knew that Jeremy and his cadre of computer nerds had dropped the video on YouTube, and they knew what they were doing. And what they were planning: They were trying to drive viewers to the show through the Internet. As I did some searching around the Internet, there were stories plastered all over the gossip Web sites, Hollywood Web sites, and celebrity scandal sites. All in one freaking night! The episode wasn't even on the air and already hundreds of thousands of people had already seen it. I was used to the days of Johnny Carson and Merv Griffin, when people like Zsa Zsa Gabor became sensations seemingly overnight, but the reality was that in those days, it actually took a long time. Even better, once you became famous, you stayed there a long time, whether you deserved it or not. Now, everything happened overnight. You went from a mild-mannered real-estate agent to a tit-flashing whore by the time you got up. Then you faded into obscurity just as quickly. One could hope.

I was getting ready to go into the office to list a few more homes that wouldn't sell for a long, long time when I heard a knock on the door, sending Knucklehead into a fit of barking. That was Knucklehead; he barked at planes, helicopters, geckos, roadrunners, birds, clouds—everything except strange men. I took a peek through the door sidelight and saw a mass of flowers sporting a woman behind it. Or was it a woman sporting a mass of flowers? I opened the door.

"Jesus Christ, Amanda. What did Ken do?" Regina barked.

"What do you mean?"

"You only get flowers like this when he's been cheating. What strumpet did you catch him with?"

"Nobody. Here . . ." I said, grabbing at the base of the flowers, trying to find something resembling stems. "Let me get those for you. Jesus, these are a lot of flowers. You mean you didn't bring them?"

"Just picked them up. What's the occasion? Someone shoot a member of The Beatles on your doorstep?"

I took the mass of flowers and laid them down on my mid-century Saarinen dining table. "They're from different people," I said, thumbing through the attached cards. "And I don't know any of them."

"Let me repeat my question: What's the occasion?"

"My Internet debut."

"Oh, the slapping thing," Regina commented.

"How do you know about that?"

"Amanda, wake up and smell the espresso. It's all over the Internet."

"Regina, since when are you all over the Internet? You hardly touched that computer I got you a month ago. I had to teach you how to use it, and when I showed you how to cruise the Net, you responded—and I quote—that you'll 'just stick to meeting men the old-fashioned way: pleasantly tight and in a dark bar.' "

"Yeah, and I stuck to that statement. You just didn't tell me there was so much porn on the Internet. And hot dating sites for older, er, mature men. I belong to so many sites with the word *silver* in the name, you'd think I was looking at a Web site for Jewish surnames."

"So even you saw me on the Internet? Holy shit."

"That's what I said when I saw your slapfest."

"Regina, it was one slap. One."

"Yeah, but what a slap it was."

"So what site did you see it on? YouTube?"

"No, on Perez Hilton's Web site. Wait a minute. I think it was on crazedbitches.com. Or bitchslap.com. Something like that."

"Regina, I don't know any of the people who sent these flowers."

"Secret admirers!" Regina gushed. "I used to have several when I worked for Paramount Studios back in '55. Montgomery Clift, Rock Hudson, James Dean."

"They were all gay. Or at least two of them were, Regina." I didn't ask her how she knew who her flowers were from if they were secret admirers. I let it ride. After all, most of Regina's stories didn't quite check out factually. I just accepted it all as the color Regina added to my life.

"They weren't always gay, Amanda. I think it was all due to those early television sets. X-rays, I tell you. Fried their balls off watching *I Love Lucy*."

"Regina, what I don't get is how all these people knew where I live. I guess I should be grateful for the adulation and attention, but at the same time, there's a creepy side to it that I'm not sure I like."

"You're not used to fame, honey," Regina said, laying her liver-spotted and bejeweled hand on mine for comfort and to assert her broad Hollywood experience. "You haven't hit the big time until someone's stalking you."

"Maybe someone is. Regina, would you check behind that yucca over there near the wall?"

Regina turned her head for a second to look, then caught herself. Great big smile. I invited her in for coffee, but she declined.

"I just came over to congratulate you."

"For the slap?"

"Yep, you're on your way, honey. You're gonna be a star."

"That's what I'm afraid of, Regina."

CHAPTER 12

Would Someone Please Shoot Me?

I had a tiny breakfast that wouldn't make my stomach stick out since we were filming again today. And the next day, and the next. With only weekends off. Today would be another pool episode, with those scenes that matched the previous day's shooting edited to make it look like they happened yesterday, and those that moved the story noticeably forward would either be super-titled as another day or be saved for the following episode. Jeremy had told us we would take between three and five days of shooting for each episode—light speed for a reality show. We would follow the same schedule each week, pumping out material for the "post" people to craft into a half-hour program. The first episode would be ready in four weeks. Again, unbelievable speed for TV show production.

It was pretty much the same as yesterday, except that no one got slapped. There were a lot of posturing, tiny bathing suits, catty retorts, rumor spreading, and Aurora and Ian sitting there watching it all like spectators in a Roman coliseum. The question was, who was going to emerge the victor? A few more days and by Thursday, we would be done shooting for this week. This would go on and on for thirteen weeks, starting Mondays and finishing each Thursday—unless we were canceled.

Some of the rumors I overheard during the filmings were somewhat surprising, but not shocking. Aleksei had penile implants, Drake owned several pairs of leather chaps, and Ian routinely had boyfriends followed by private investigators. Other revelations later sent me to urbandictionary.com to look them up since I had no idea what snowballing, an Alaskan fire dragon, or a rusty trombone were. Trust me, you don't want to know.

A month went by, filled with a little more drama each time. There was a drunken brawl between Aleksei and Gilles, Ian stormed off the set several times, and Drake destroyed a fair amount of household items those four weeks. Manufactured drama for the most part . . . just what I had predicted.

And before you knew it, the first episode was ready to air on Sunday night. In a really good time slot. The program schedulers at the network obviously had a lot of faith riding on their decision. They felt our little show was going to be a big hit. Alex and Regina came over to my house to celebrate episode one with a nice bottle of champagne and my new fifty-five–inch flat-screen TV.

"I'm so glad you got rid of that last goddamn TV, Amanda," Regina said as I poured her another glass of bubbly. "This one is so much nicer." Today's T-shirt she wore read: FUCK ME, I'M FAMOUS.

"I wouldn't talk, Regina. Yours is still housed in a Mediterranean cabinet. How old is it?"

"Twenty, twenty-five years old."

"I didn't think TVs lasted that long," Alex remarked.

"Well, it's not like this fancy one you got, but you can still make out colors and shapes on it."

"Shhh," Alex warned as the show came on.

The opening started with ominous music that slowly built over footage of Ian Forbes and his hair empire while a narrator laid down the premise of the show. This was followed, like any reality show, with blaring rock music to get people excited. After the titles, each of the show's cast members got their five seconds of fame as they were highlighted. Some cast members turned slowly toward the camera like they were on a human-sized turntable. Some leered naughtily at the camera. Aleksei was shot toasting the audience with a glass of champagne.

Alex and Regina watched the entire show with rapt attention, amazed at how much of the "artwork" in Ian's home had to be pixilated because it was too obscene for television. But the time you watched a few minutes of the show, you would've sworn you had cataracts. When it came to the end of the episode and my peep show, the two of them sat with mouths wide open even though they had seen it dozens of times on the Internet.

"Your bazongas are huge on a wide-screen TV!" Regina said, downing the contents of her champagne flute. "Good thing you don't have a 3-D TV. Those things could've poked my eyes out!"

Up came the reaction shots, followed by Aurora, who wrapped up the show by giving a brutally honest assessment of the guys:

They're rude, crass, untrustworthy, and self-centered. When they're not trying to outslime each other, then they're texting and not connecting with another human being in a meaning-

ful way. I don't see how some of them are going to make it with their toxic personalities. Now, I know that Ian is not easy to get along with. He's tough, egotistical, ruthless, paranoid, and could stand to lose a few pounds, so I need to find someone who could put up with his antics and his paunchy abdomen. But this is going to be a struggle to find a guy with some sort of integrity. I refuse to lower the bar here, and it's pretty low as it is. Drake and David are the standouts so far. David can be a little sarcastic and high-and-mighty, but he has honesty. And Drake, he's loyal, hardworking, doesn't get involved in the petty interactions of the others, and like David, he seems to be honest. He's a bit dark, but I think that characteristic appeals to Ian as well.

The show cut to scenes of upcoming episodes (even though they weren't even filmed), most of which were assumptions of where Jeremy and the editors were sure the show would head in the future. The editors cleverly used dramatic reaction shots with verbiage that could have been used no matter what ensued. It was like a fortune-teller or astrologer, giving predictions so vague and adaptable, the listener would read more into them than they actually deserved. The next-episode scenes were followed by credits that surprised me. The number of people who put on the show was far greater than I had seen at the filmings, so I wondered what cost savings Jeremy gained by using an unscripted format. The credits revealed, like with any TV program or movie made in Hollywood, that everyone within a 100-mile radius got a credit on the show, whether they styled our hair or walked Jeremy's dog.

I waited a moment to ask what Alex and Regina thought.

"Fuckin' great, Amanda. That bitch slap is going to make

you famous. Fuckin' great," Regina said, finishing her champagne.

"And you?" I asked, looking at Alex and realizing that his reply was the only one that mattered.

"You did great, kid. I'm proud of you," he replied.

I studied the tone and inflection of his comment, and searched his face again. Alex had a terrific poker face, but I could see behind the mask. He thought I did a great job. Mostly. I could see the ten percent that wasn't on board. I felt like a failure. Then, like me reading Alex, he read my thoughts.

"Hey, hey, what's that face for?"

"What?" I said, lying to him.

"I can see what's going through that head of yours. Amanda, you're on a reality show. It's not *Masterpiece Theatre*. That's okay." He grabbed my chin delicately and turned my face to look directly into his eyes. "Y-o-u a-r-e o-n t-e-l-e-v-i-s-i-o-n, Amanda. That's a billion-to-one shot. And you stole the first show. Stole it! And you kept your dignity. So stop feeling sorry for yourself. You aced it."

I believed him. Mostly.

Alex continued, sensing that he was on a roll with his ego boosting. "On the first show, you've established your character and it's a hit. It resonates with viewers. You're the voice of reason on this morally topsy-turvy program of conniving gold diggers. There's almost no one on the show who's likable, but you are. You stand up to the bullshit. You fight back. People like you."

"That's right, Amanda. I really liked you . . . rooted for you," Regina slipped in.

"Oh, that's just the two of you saying that to make me feel better."

Just then my iPhone, which was on *silent*, started jumping and buzzing on the tabletop like a cicada on a hot July afternoon. And it didn't stop. I went over, wondering which client was now having a drama-queen episode. I looked at the mass of text messages, and there was a list as long as your arm. Friends, cousins, clients, coworkers were all sending messages of congratulations. They loved me! I showed the messages to Alex and Regina, who quickly scanned them and nodded their heads in approval.

"Amanda?" Alex sang slowly. "I think the people have spoken."

CHAPTER 13

And What Are Your Plans for That Cucumber?

The next night, I found myself driving to our local bowling alley. Monday night was the gay bowling league. I was on the only straight team. Us four girls: Jerri, Samantha, Regina Belle, and me. What brought us together is that all our husbands turned out to be gay. Well, in Regina's case, one of several, making her batting average better than the rest of us simply because she had been married more times. So, since we loved the company of gay men, we figured it wouldn't hurt to be surrounded by them holding sixteen-pound balls. We even had our team name embroidered on our bowling shirts: THE FAG HAGS, in very fancy script. In sequins. Strangely enough, we stuck out like a sore thumb in a sea of gay men, transvestites, one transsexual, and the Sisters of Perpetual Indulgence. They rarely wore their official transvestite nun habits, owing to the fateful day when Sister Way Too Much's habit got caught in the ball return and she was almost dragged into the bowels of the machine. From that day on, only facial makeup and short headpieces were worn by the Sisters. *Very* short, I might add.

When I walked in, I kept my head low. I wanted to slip in quietly with as few people noticing me as was possible.

That plan went into the shitter when several of the bowlers recognized me immediately and began a standing ovation. Those who didn't join in craned their necks to see what all the commotion was about. You would have thought I rolled a 300 game.

Right then, I did the most uncharacteristic thing I'd ever done in my life. I waved my hand with an Elizabeth II royal wave and followed it with a bow. This was so not me. All my life, I'd avoided being seen, being recognized, being photographed. And here I was, sweeping in the praise and adoration as the waves washed over me. So this is what it felt like to be a celebrity. I liked it.

Several of the guys clustered around me, gushing about my performance in the premiere episode of *Things Are a Bit Iffy*. As I changed into my bowling shoes, fans lobbed questions at me about my first episode.

"Was the slap real or was it staged?"

"Did you wish you hit Gilles harder?"

"Who are you going to punch next?"

"Did you have a boob job?" (I didn't take offense at this last question since it was asked by Carla de Rossi, the league's only transsexual.) The initial adoration and congratulations eventually died down, but throughout the night, men would drift by or shout "great slap" to me while I was waiting my turn to bowl. It must have had an effect on my bowling, because I rolled a 220, 231, and 267. It would all be forgotten in the morning, I told myself.

It wasn't.

I didn't realize how much my celebrity had spread. Videos posted on YouTube containing parts of the show were nearing 1,200,000 views by the time I got up. When I walked into my local supermarket and entered the vegetable and fruit section around 10 A.M., it really hit me how my life was changing—whether I liked it or not. Granted, I was wearing mini-stilettos, skintight cigarette capri pants, and a low-cut white linen blouse—just the kind of outfit you would wear to pick over zucchinis. As I made my way around the onion and potato table, I could feel dozens of pairs of eyes boring holes in my back.

I moved onto the lettuce and cabbage section, and I was keenly aware that not only was I being watched, but whispered about. I went about my business, thumping a cantaloupe, squeezing a vine-ripened tomato, when a man provocatively holding two casaba melons approached me slyly, puckering up enough to send off a seductive air kiss that said, "I want to get my hands on your tomatoes." I ignored him—the price of celebrity.

But my adoring fans weren't done with me yet. A man standing near me, who was sneaking quick sideways glances, whispered discreetly, "Slap me."

I looked at him briefly, not sure I had heard what I heard. I went back to my Roma tomatoes.

"Slap me, Amanda."

This I couldn't let go. "Excuse me?" I said.

"Slap me. Step on my nuts with the heel of those stilettos."

"Do I know you?" I asked, and turned away.

"I want you to violate me with this yam," he said, brandishing a rather oversized tuberous root vegetable.

"That's a sweet potato."

"Well, it's a yam, too," he replied defensively.

"Yams are from Africa, Asia, and Latin America. This is a sweet potato. They're from completely different botanical families."

"Potato potah-to. I want you to ram it into me, Amanda. Make me your bitch."

At first I was put off by this man's appalling lack of knowledge of the origins of basic foods. But my encounter with him had taken a more ominous turn. It wasn't the sexual component that disturbed me. From the time I was old enough to know what was going on and had breasts big enough to cause male heads to turn, I knew I was being hit on by men from time to time. Creepy fact, but those were the times. There were no sexual harassment laws, no predator laws, or women to stand up for themselves when I was growing up. Of course, it was a great improvement over my grandmother's time, when she claimed that they left the female babies to the wolves in her Lithuanian village because they weren't worth as much as a man. So I accepted the evolution that had occurred in human thought, however small that it was.

No, what really bothered me was the fact that from the instant this man used my name, he was acting as if he actually knew me—that he felt comfortable enough to be intimate with me. I knew a line had been crossed. It was unfortunate. I wanted adoring fans, the operative word here being adoring. Adoring meant people standing at a respectful and reverential distance, whispering how much they wanted to be like me—no, to be me—and perhaps snapping a picture to show the folks back home while throwing large bags of gold, frankincense, and myrrh in my general direction. But it concerned me that fans wouldn't always follow the rules I had laid down in my mind. I discovered that I should be nice to all of my fans, but I shouldn't be too nice to any of them.

"Get down on your knees," I said, surprising myself.

"What?" the startled yam . . . I mean, sweet-potato–wielding man replied.

"Didn't you hear me? I said get down on your knees while I finish shopping," I stated firmly, extending my index finger with the blood-red nail toward the floor, where I expected this man to grovel. "I have more shopping to do. I expect to find you here when I come back!" I said, raising my voice a bit at the end for emphasis. He never got fully down on his knees, and as soon as I was far enough away, he dropped the sweet potato and ran out of the store.

A woman who was watching all this transpire from a distance drifted toward me. She decided to comment on what she had just seen.

"Men!"

"You said it, sister."

"I recognized you as Amanda Thorne on *Things Are a Bit Iffy*."

"That's me," I said, thrusting out my hand to shake. She grabbed my hand and pumped it like an enthusiastic candidate for governor.

"So glad to meet you. When I saw you slap that little French bitch on the TV show, I felt a stab of sisterhood. We don't need to take that from the male patriarchy."

"Er, yeah."

"I mean, men have been oppressing us since we walked out of caves and realized we could do more than breed and cook."

Now, I'm a feminist to a very large extent. I still have my EVE WAS FRAMED bumper sticker on the back of my Toyota

Land Cruiser. I still admire Gloria Steinem, mostly. But when I hear a woman making remarks that involve words like *oppression, patriarchy,* or *forced castration,* it's too much for me. I mean, I like men. I like being fucked by them. I was married to one, for gosh sakes. Of course, he turned out to be gay. But he is still a man, no matter where his penis has been.

"I'm not sure he was oppressing me per se. I think he's just a bitchy French queen. An equal opportunity offender, if you will. Now, if you'll excuse me, I have a kumquat that's calling me. A pleasure to meet you."

I left her standing there, unsure whether I was a bitch, really had fruit to buy, or was too much of a celebrity to bother with the unwashed masses. And to tell you the truth, I wasn't sure what I was just then either.

CHAPTER 14

What Does A Scotsman Have Hidden Under His Kilt?

"**W**ell, Toviah broke the code of ethics for models—he smiled on the runway. Everyone knows you're supposed to be devoid of emotion, thought, and feeling during a show. I mean, no wonder he can't find work. He did it to himself," David warned.

We were all seated around Ian's cavernous living room, cameras rolling while we waited for Aleksei to arrive. In the beginning, Jeremy insisted that everyone be present when we began shooting, but two things changed his mind. Having people show up naturally was, well, more real. Plus, these were gay men. Correction, these were gay men who were models—they rarely showed up on time. When Aleksei finally did enter the room, something was out of place about him: He was wearing a hat instead of sporting a new hair color or style.

"What's with the hat?" Ian asked.

Without saying a word, Aleksei removed his cap to reveal a bald scalp that looked like it had been scrubbed with a steel wool pad. His scalp was an angry red.

"Someone put depilatory in my shampoo. I felt it when I

was shampooing—the burning—but by the time I figured out what was happening, it was too late."

"That's too bad, Aleksei. Maybe it was just cheap shampoo," David replied with just a hint of a smile on his face.

"And maybe it was just someone cheap who put that hair remover into my shampoo?" Aleksei fired back.

"I don't know what you're talking about, Aleksei. I have no reason to sabotage you or anyone on this show. I will win this thing fair and square. I don't need to resort to childish tricks. Why don't you wear your wigs, then?"

"Someone cut those up as well."

Just then, Gilles joined us in the living room. Naked. Yes, he was huge. I mean, huge. And second, he was definitely European. Now I understood Ian's attraction to Gilles.

"Well, someone act like a child," Gilles joined in. He held up a pair of pants to reveal a large, ragged hole in the seat area. All my pants, ze swim suits, zhorts . . . all zeese holes!" He sat down dejectedly on a white cotton duck sofa. "I need to look good for the camera."

I made a mental note not to sit on that sofa again.

"Gilles," I started, "in case you hadn't noticed, we're filming here. I know you might live in the Marais in Paris, but here in Palm Springs, we wear clothes . . . sometimes. Or at least underwear. Some of us . . . especially when we're in front of cameras."

I knew perfectly clear why Gilles had come into the filming naked. Partly, he was French. But mainly, he was showing off his assets—something that Ian didn't fail to notice. Nor I. I had to hand it to him, he had a huge cock. Low-hanging balls. Pubic hair that needed a trim, but other than that . . . I understood that women weren't supposed to think about such things, let alone talk about them, but there was something about dicks being so primal. The undeniable masculinity of a man. And yes, I was horny. Ken was still caring for his mother and I hadn't gotten laid in weeks. Believe me, nothing else about Gilles turned me on, but his dick was reminding me that I needed to get laid. And soon.

"I think someone is trying to send a message," I added.

"I agree," David chipped in. "You could drive a Cadillac Escalade through that hole."

Gilles agreed. "Zhoost look at zeese hole," he said, holding up the violated pair of pants again.

"I wasn't talking about that hole, Gilles."

Gilles threw the pair of pants on the floor in disgust. "I don't know why you must attack Gilles so much."

"Because you throw the blood in the water yourself. A shark can't say no."

"I just don't know why they don't finish this contest seeze day and declare me zee winner. If I don't win soon, I will have to zell my body on the street."

"Gilles, you can't sell from an empty pushcart," I said, lobbing in a zinger that was thankfully caught on film. I don't know why I said that. It was like some comic persona inside of me had taken control of my tongue and made me say it. Normally, I would just stay out of conflicts of any sort. An argument between a store manger and a customer: I'd leave the store. Between two drivers over a parking space? I'd hit the gas and peel out of there. I guess my growing fame was making me fearless. Or, it was making me crave attention. I wasn't sure if this was a good thing. Maybe I was just getting in touch with my inner asshole.

No matter how you looked at it, the gloves were off early today.

"I have something to say," Keith announced with great importance, like he was going to drop a bomb, but considering all the manufactured drama on this show, I was skeptical. "I am Ian's son."

Okay, it was a bomb. A big one.

No one knew what to say for the longest time, but I could guess the two main thoughts that were going through everyone's head: *I just lost out on $350 million,* and *Ian screwed his own son. Ewwwww!*

Ian sat silently, looking like a deer caught in the headlights of a Winnebago. No one immediately challenged Keith as to the truth to his story, so he launched an explanation of his own. Me, I was just interested. The guys, however, wanted to know if it was true. After all, it might give Keith a claim to Ian's fortune in some twisted way or, even worse, Ian might get all touchy-feely over the prospect of a son and give him a big piece of the action out of deference to a bloodline.

Keith took a big breath, then commenced with his story. "My mother, Ena, was married to Ian a long time ago in Scotland. They both started a small hair salon in Glasgow that became somewhat successful. Ena and Ian had no children for a long time. As time went on, my mother was unable to control her drinking, and Ian eventually forced her out of the business, which Ian eventually sold before he divorced Ena and moved to America. What my father"—he pointed to Ian as if it was an accepted fact—"didn't know was that my mother was pregnant with me at about the time Ian left her. Ena, fearing the stigma of being a single mother, kept the truth about me quiet as long as she could. By the time I was born, Ian had left the country for Los Angeles. For years, my mother struggled with her addiction and tried to earn a living in a hair salon, but eventually she succumbed to liver cancer and died when I was eight years old. I then went to live with relatives of my mother until I was eighteen. All the time, my mother had drilled into my head her various plans for revenge on my father for abandoning the two of us. I grew up being taught how to use people, manipulate them, and how to find Ian and get close to him. Well, I made my way to the U.S. and wormed my way into Ian's life by working on my body and buffing up, showing up at clubs Ian was likely to visit, and the plan worked. But there, I changed direction from the plans that my mother laid. Instead of killing him or trying to ruin him, I fell in love with him. So here I am. I confess."

"I must disagree wiss that story," Gilles chimed in.

"How so?" Keith countered.

"You said you work on the body. Buffing up. That is where I disagree. To me, you are a sack of rocks."

"*Salope.*"

I was impressed. Keith knew French.

Aurora, feeling the need to referee a bit, stepped in.

"Ian, is Keith telling the truth?"

"It could be. Oh, what's the big deal? I barely touched him."

Aurora again, "You were married?"

"Yes, to Ena. What Keith is saying is true. That was a long time ago."

"About how long ago?"

"Twenty . . . um," Ian said, stopping himself once the numbers added up. Yes, Keith is probably my son."

"But wait a minute," I said, jumping in, not wanting to be out of the limelight too much. After all, I wanted to stay on the show . . . I had bills to pay. "You don't have the same surnames."

"My last name was Forbes. I had it changed before I left for America so that Ian wouldn't suspect anything as I courted him. And I have the paperwork to prove it."

"Well, that blows a hole in my objection," I conceded.

I recapped what happened on the show that day to Alex over dinner at my house.

"So Ian doesn't really care that he slept with his son?"

"Not really. He said he's done worse."

"How can you do worse than that?"

"Ian had twins as lovers once."

"Ugh!"

"Fraternal. That's why Ian said it didn't bother him."

"That was his answer?" Alex answered, flabbergasted.

"Well, he also pointed out that he's dying. He doesn't really care."

"Amanda, this development is really going to throw a monkey wrench into the whole works. This might make the show unnecessary. Ian might have his heartstrings pulled by Keith because of the family connection and leave everything to him. What is Jeremy thinking about all of this?"

"Jeremy? He's loving it. Now, in addition to bitching, treachery, greed, and hatred, he has incest and a huge target for the rest of the guys to aim at. Keith might as well just wear a T-shirt with a huge bull's-eye on it."

"From what you've told me, Amanda, when it comes to snide comments, their aim is pretty good."

"It's not the comments I'm worried about. They don't leave a hole like a bullet can."

CHAPTER 15

A Twisted Game of Twister

The next morning, we assembled in Ian's living room to get ready for another day of shooting. As usual, we started at 6 A.M. since there was so much to set up, everyone had to be made up, and it was all done so that we could start shooting around 10:30 when the deep shadows of morning and evening weren't around. Scenes had to be matched for lighting too. I never knew that even in small productions like *Things Are a Bit Iffy*, it took so much time to prepare what was supposed to end up looking so real and spontaneous. The entire cast was present, except for Keith, who, as usual, was the last to show up.

Apparently, no one got a lot of sleep last night. At around 2:30 A.M., one of Ian's penis sculptures slipped off its base at the top of the stairs and went tumbling down the stairwell, taking several other penises with it in its tumble. The noise could've waked the dead, Aurora reported. Ian, David, Drake, and Marcus eventually came running downstairs over the commotion, but, of course, it was Ian who made the loudest noise over the incident. Ian actually wailed over the loss of his work of art since he claimed that it was a scale model of Jack Wrangler's cock. Jack Wrangler was one of the most famous gay porn stars in the 1970s. Anyway, by the time the guys got Ian calmed down, got him to swallow an Ambien, and escorted him back to his bedroom, a good half-hour had passed and everyone eventually went back to sleep.

But now that it was morning, Jeremy was getting visibly upset that Keith hadn't showed yet.

"David, could you be a dear and go fetch Keith? We need to start shooting ASAP!" he said. As soon as David padded upstairs, Jeremy continued, "Okay, to bring you all up to speed, the last time we had Keith reveal he was Ian's son and Ian had incestuous sex with him at one time or another. We also had the sabotaging of Gilles's clothing and David's hair, the uncovering of Aleksei's penile implants, blah, blah blah. Let's keep those events in mind as we start today. We'll want some reactions about the incest thing."

A minute later, David came back down the stairs, flung himself back in the chair he had just vacated, and picked up the copy of *Numéro* magazine that he had been reading earlier without saying a word.

"Well . . . ?" Ian spoke up. "Is Keith coming down or are we going to have to start without him?"

"If I were you, I'd start without him. He's dead," David pronounced, flipping another page in his magazine.

"What do you mean dead?" Ian asked, scratching for an answer. "You mean, like dead to the world, like in a deep sleep?"

"No, like dead-dead. Like not living. Not breathing."

"Are you sure?" Ian continued, not believing what his ears were hearing. The rest of the cast sat with their mouths stuck open, showing hundreds of blindingly white teeth. "How can you be so sure?"

"Well, Ian"—David put his magazine down with an annoying slam onto the coffee table—"he's lying there on the floor like he'd been playing a game of Twister by himself. I think he probably overdosed."

"Why would you think that, David?" Ian asked with more than a little irritation showing.

"Because he's a dealer."

"He is not!" Ian struck back. "My son is not a dealer."

"Yes, he is, Ian—or *was*! I'm sorry to break the news to you, but Keith is a dealer . . . and not a very good one either. Bad drugs. The shitty stuff. Ian, his clubs haven't been doing so well, so he's been supplementing his income by selling drugs in his clubs. He's been supplying a lot of models too. Female and MALE!"

Several sets of eyes hit the floor or wandered off into space, trying to look as innocent as possible.

"Uh, guys," I said, butting in. "We seem to be forgetting that someone is dead upstairs. Maybe. Probably."

I got up and was followed by everyone else in the room—except David. I guess he had made up his mind, had seen enough, and seemed more interested in a spread in a French women's fashion magazine than confirming whether Keith was taking a long nap or ready to push up a whole lot of daisies. When we got to Keith's room, I was shocked by what I saw. I expected to see Keith sitting as if he had fallen asleep in a comfy chair on a snowy afternoon. This was not the case. Keith's body was lying on the floor, bent back in a painful arch like some kind of sadistic Pilates exercise. We're talking painful. Even worse was the expression on his face. He looked like he had died crying, no, bawling his eyes out, his mouth in a downturned scowl. This was not a quiet death.

Ian rushed around me and tried to pick Keith up and cradle him, but Keith was stiffer than an Episcopalian singing a black spiritual.

"My son, my son!" Ian wailed, holding Keith for the appropriate amount of time, then letting him drop to the floor. "I just can't take it. Why is it that I always have to bear so much sorrow? I am retiring to my room now and taking another sleeping pill. No one is to disturb me until lunch."

Ian left and the rest of us huddled around the doorway, not sure of what to do. Jeremy's assistant, Tony, called out from downstairs: "I've called 911 and they're on their way."

Having experience with several bodies in my listings or at my own house, I stepped in and decided to take charge.

"Okay, we've disturbed the crime scene enough. We need to leave the area and go downstairs."

No one moved an inch.

"What's the matter, guys?" I pleaded.

"We're scared," Aleksei reported, taking a quick consensus from the crowd.

"Why?"

"Because Keith was murdered. The killer may be still in the house."

"How do you know he was murdered?" I asked, lying to myself when I knew full well that Keith was put out of action for his ties to Ian.

Gilles, oddly—and thankfully—silent for the longest time, spoke up, "Someone want to get Keith out of the contest. So, pop!" he said, pointing his finger like a gun, then shooting it.

"Let's all go down together; then we'll all be safe."

Gilles, not known for having tremendous insights into life—or anything, for that matter—had made an astute observation. "The killer, he ees one of us, perhaps?"

I hated to agree with anything that Gilles said, but in this case, I had to admit to myself that he was probably right.

Several police cars arrived within minutes, probably owing to the fact that the dispatcher recognized Ian's address from the 911 call. Ian was a constant irritant in Palm Springs due to his caustic nature, but he was also a big contributor to police charities. Mostly as a payoff to keep his partiers from being arrested for drugs or explicit public sexual acts.

Several uniformed policemen entered, followed by a plainclothes detective. Dating a homicide detective gives you a little insight into how the police operate. Plus, this one recognized me.

"Amanda! Fancy meeting you here!"

I fished around in my memory and hoped I got the name right. "Jerry? Jerry Hallander?"

I got a great big hug from the detective.

"I haven't seen you since you were brought into the police station for breaking and entering."

"The charges were dropped, Jerry."

"That's right. You and your gay ex. You were trying to find out if that Realtor, Mary Dodge, killed Doc Winters. Wow! It seems like ages. So, what's going on here?"

I took him into the kitchen, sat him down, and proceeded to tell him the whole story. He was taking it all down on his iPad. He then started upstairs, beckoning to me with his finger to follow him. I did, leaving the rest of the cast downstairs and bewildered as to why I was getting special treatment.

"So, Jerry, why are you bringing me up here with you? To what do I owe this honor?

"I need someone who's on the inside. I need you to fill me in on the personalities here."

"Jerry, they're male models. Personality isn't the first word that comes to mind."

"You know what I mean. Who's who, etcetera."

"You mean who's doing who? The answer: everyone."

"Well, nothing's changed here. We're always getting calls about guys screwing on the lawn of Ian's estate."

"Jerry, the walls here must be eight feet tall and the vegetation is higher than that. You can't see anything from the street."

"You can when you're on the celebrity tour bus. It's a double-decker."

"Oh," I said. "I guess the tourists got some photos that the folks back in Kansas won't believe."

"That's not the half of it, Amanda. Sometimes there are guys screwing, sometimes there's someone dressed in a rubber catsuit tied between palm trees. Whipping, flogging, piss parties. You name it, we've gotten complaints about it."

"I had no idea," I replied as we walked down the hall to Keith's room. "You see, Jerry, that's the problem with being a straight woman in a gay town. Great parties and fun bars, but you always feel like an outsider."

"You're upset because you don't get invited to a piss party?"

"No, not that. It's just that life is going on around here and I'm not on the inside track."

"I'm a straight cop in a very gay city. How do you think I feel? But I get on with my life. I don't get invited to a lot of parties since there are either drugs there or people are drinking and driving. People treat me like they've invited someone's mother to a party. Not fun."

Normally, Jerry wouldn't even leave a blip on my sexual radar screen, but he had changed since I had last seen him. He lost some weight, put on some muscles, and stopped having his gray hair dyed, leaving it to go my second favorite color after jet black: salt and pepper. He wore a really nicely tailored suit. In short, he had climbed quite a few numbers on the hot meter.

We reached Keith's room. Jerry peered in, then whistled.

"Boy, I haven't seen this in a long time," he said.

"Seen what? A murder? You're a homicide detective."

"No, strychnine. Nasty stuff."

"You can tell just by looking at him?"

"Amanda, this isn't conclusive, but it has all the signs of strychnine. The jackknifed back, the eyes wide open, and the grimace on the face. Looks like he's been dead since late last night. So you think one of the guys downstairs killed this . . ." he said, looking at his iPad again, ". . . Keith because he was the son of Ian Forbes?"

"*Possible* heir, Jerry."

Jerry stood at the doorway, avoiding going in just yet until the crime scene unit arrived. He scanned the room slowly, over and over, looking at the carpet, the windows, drawers, bed. I scanned the room, too, but didn't see anything that looked suspicious. Well, except for the glass on the nightstand, which probably delivered the poison.

"Look at the glass," Jerry commented.

"What's so unusual about it?"

"It has the faintest tinge of red. Very, very faint."

"And that means what? Keith often drank cranberry juice because he was susceptible to kidney stones."

"Orange juice is a better antidote to stones."

"Oh, so you're a doctor too?" I joked, realizing that I was starting to flirt a bit.

"Just a detective. Amanda, is there someone here who manages the property?"

"Drake Whittemore. He manages the estate, inside and out."

"Excellent. I have a question to ask him."

"He's sitting downstairs."

"Before we go down, has he had relations with Ian Forbes?"

"You're not a very good detective, Jerry. All of the men downstairs have pillowed Ian at one time or another. With the exception of the show's staff . . . you know, the director, cameramen, etcetera. Actually, I can't say that's completely true. There's a lot of sex that goes on around here."

"Gotcha. Let's go find Drake."

We descended the stairs, and as I followed Jerry, I eyed the entire cast to see if there was guilt visible on anyone's face.

"Which one of you is Drake?" Jerry asked.

"I am," Drake responded.

"Could I ask you a few questions in the . . . er, kitchen, wherever that is?"

"Sure."

As Drake got up to lead the way, Gilles piped up. "Oh, oh. Zee trouble begins."

Drake, as usual, didn't respond to the daily comments and quips that sailed around Ian's home like an erratic parrot.

We entered the kitchen and I offered a seat to Drake. Drake declined, preferring to stand. I was curious. What was Jerry looking for? I tried to figure out where his path of logic was taking him, but I couldn't yet discern anything.

"Drake, are there pocket gophers on the estate?"

Jerry's question caught me totally off guard. Either he was very good or just crazy.

"They're all over the place," Drake admitted. "They're driving Ian crazy since his *cha-cha heels* sink into their holes when he's walking on the grounds."

"Okay . . ." Jerry replied, discerning a bit of scorn in Drake's voice. "Drake, do you keep gopher poison here on the estate?"

"In the potting shed. I'll show you."

Drake led the way to a building on the back of the garage. He opened the door to the shed and led us inside.

"There's no lock on the shed door?" Ken asked.

"No," Drake replied. "Why lock it? It's full of pots and garden tools. Nothing worth stealing. Besides, no one ever goes in here but me. No one that I know of. Can you imagine Ian or any of his playthings getting their hands dirty?"

"I see your point," Ken replied.

The shed was neat beyond belief. The shelves were orderly to a compulsiveness, with labeled bottles and labeled drawers. Nothing seemed to be out of place. Jerry slowly took in the room, then pointed toward a large white, plastic, spike-shaped container lying on a high shelf, neatly on its side.

"Drake, is that the container where the gopher poison is stored?"

"You mean this?" Drake responded, reaching for the container, only to have his hands stopped in mid-flight by Jerry's hand.

"You don't need to touch it, Drake."

Drake, having been to Yale, was no dummy. "You suspect that Keith was poisoned? Shit! Well . . . you insert the spike into the ground until you feel it hit a gopher tunnel; then you pull it out, drop some pellets into the hole, and cover it up."

"Drake, now it looks like you run a very tight ship here. Can you tell me if anything is missing . . . or out of place?"

Drake looked around a few seconds, but it seemed more to placate the detective's questioning. "Nope, everything is where it's supposed to be."

"You seem awfully sure of that."

Drake smiled. "I can tell. Believe me. I'm orderly to the point of being insane."

"Okay, Drake. Thank you for your time. You can return to the house. Oh, and even after the crime lab people have gone through the shed, could you not touch anything for a few weeks? Thanks."

"Sure. You're welcome. Anything I can do to help."

After Drake had gone, I started with my questions.

"So gopher poison is made of strychnine, huh?"

"Yes, blended with barley grain or anything enticing to gophers."

"So does strychnine have a taste?"

"It's incredibly bitter."

I inched a bit further. "So it wouldn't be tasted if it were in something strong like cranberry juice?"

Jerry, still looking around the shed, put his finger on his nose and pointed the other free index finger at me. "You might make a good detective one day. Keep it up. If it does turn out to be strychnine—which I would bet that it was— the killer knew enough that he had to hide the taste."

"And even more telling, the killer had to know that Keith regularly drank cranberry juice because of his kidneys."

"And . . . ?" Jerry prompted me, seeing if I could make the leap to the next clue.

"Uh . . . Uh . . . you went to the well too many times, Jerry."

"Someone would have to grind up the gopher powder somewhere to make the poison. So somewhere on the estate, maybe, there's a container that was used in the commission of the crime. If the killer is smart, that container is probably in someone else's trashcan miles from here by now, but you never know. So we need to stop all garbage going out immediately."

I looked around the room, wondering if any of the containers here were used to prepare Keith's lethal beverage. There was an old-fashioned watering can, a small, dented metal paint bucket, a few old plastic food containers that Drake had washed out and reused—it was hard to tell. I guess that only the forensics unit would know for sure.

"I wish I could hire Drake to organize my house. Look at this place! Everything in its proper place, everything labeled, nothing out of place, nothing broken. Perfect."

Jerry looked around the room again and commented, "A bit on the *anal* side, isn't he?"

"I'd be careful how you use that word around here if I were you, Detective."

CHAPTER 16

The Pocket Gopher Did It

Jerry questioned everyone separately. Just about everyone was up fairly late. Aleksei was busy coloring his newly grown, but very short hair stubble so that it would be ready for the day's shooting. David was performing fellatio on a nearly comatose Ian, then returned to his room to look through a stack of fashion magazines. Gilles was on his computer watching some of the French fashion shows on YouTube. Aurora was going over notes that she had written up about the men on the show. And Ian, as usual, couldn't sleep and took an Ambien and crashed until Lance Greenly shook him out of his coma when the sculpture fell down the stairs. Lance was up most of the night working on financial projections for Ian's company for next year. His story got real interesting when he said he went down to the kitchen at around 1:30 to get a Red Bull and saw Keith coming out of Aleksei's room with his shirt off. Everyone else said they went to bed by 1 A.M. and didn't get up and didn't leave their rooms until the stairway incident.

"It's amazing how the sculpture fell just about the time I estimate Keith was probably going through his convulsions from the strychnine, isn't it?" Jerry confided to me.

"So someone knocked over the penis to cover the noise from Keith's swan song?"

"You got it. I'm sure Keith would have been making a lot of noise thrashing around when the strychnine really hit him."

"Since you know a scary amount about poisons, Detective Hallander," I said, "how long would it take from the moment he ingested the poison to the time it really started to hit him?"

"Ten to twenty minutes after ingesting it, more if on a full stomach."

"So that means he would have taken the strychnine about two A.M. Maybe a little earlier."

"About that time."

"Which means he probably came down to the kitchen around one-thirty to one forty-five or two A.M. to get some cranberry juice. Oh shit! It could still be there in the refrigerator!"

"Relax, Amanda. I already had the juice rounded up for the lab. It seems kinda chancy, though, on the killer's part. Someone else could have drank it."

"No, not really. Keith wrote his name on the jug of cranberry juice. Everyone in the cast is doing that since they're all living here like one big happy family."

"Except that one member of this family is highly dysfunctional." Jerry snorted.

"And that would be different from any family how?" I replied. "Well, Lance's trip to the kitchen was convenient too. Just in time to have the opportunity to poison Keith's juice."

CHAPTER 17

The $how Must Go On

The cast managed to pull itself together as Jeremy called an emergency meeting in Ian's billiard room later that morning.

"I've been on the phone all morning with executives from the network. First . . ." he said, turning toward Ian. "They would like to send their condolences for the de . . . the . . . whatever happened to Keith. So . . . they're extremely sad and sorry and everything. Now, the reason I've gathered you all here is to discuss the future of the show."

Several members of the cast scoffed at what they were hearing.

"Now, now, before you say no to the idea of going on, I want you to hear me out. I think that if we were to go and throw away all our hard work, I want you to first consider Keith and what this show meant to him."

Everyone looked at each other, flashes of guilt briefly passing over their faces even though Jeremy's statement was as suspect as a holy relic.

Drake spoke up, "Jeremy, I know that you have reasons to want the show to go on, but I think I speak for the rest of us in saying that we're all too filled with inconsolable grief to want to go on."

Jeremy maneuvered like a mongoose squaring off with a cobra. "Drake, I really want to thank you for airing those very *personal* emotions, but we have to consider what Keith would have wanted, and I think if he were here today, he would have wanted this show to continue. Remember, Keith was in show business, and you know what they say: 'The show must go on.' "

"Keith designed nightclubs and texted people to get them into those clubs," Drake corrected Jeremy.

"Drake?" Jeremy continued, rushing up to Drake and getting in his face . . . lovingly. "Drake, Drake, Drake, Drake. What are nightclubs but show business? You've got lights"— he emphasized by pointing up at imaginary lights— "music"—he cupped his hand to his ear—"and PEOPLE! It's all showbiz!"

Several of the guys shook their heads in agreement. Like a fundamentalist preacher, Jeremy paused for a few calculated seconds, then changed gears.

"Now that we've got Keith's wishes to think about, I want to say something else that you might want to consider. I'm as upset as you are and I want to always respect Keith's memory—but the studio executives are saying that this latest development could send our little show into the ratings stratosphere. Higher than it's climbed already. Even higher than *American Idol!*" he said as he threw in an are-you-with-me face, complete with raised eyebrows. "Think about it. You will be household names which could lead you—I don't know—anywhere after this show. A-N-Y-W-H-E-R-E!"

There was complete silence as what Jeremy uttered insinuated itself into our heads.

Ian, a man used to getting a fair amount of press (not all of it favorable), swallowed Jeremy's bait—hook, line, and sinker. "Jeremy's right," he said enthusiastically. "Keith would have wanted us to go on."

This sentiment was echoed by the other members of the cast, including one that sort of shocked me: Aurora. But as I learned, the more we filmed, celebrity—no matter how petty and short-lived—had a power and momentum of its own. It was like a train, and once started, it was hard to stop. Plus, these people didn't want the ride to stop. And to be totally honest, I wasn't sure I wanted that either. I mean, why not make a little more money, grab a little more fame, and get a lot more business? It's not like any of us could bring Keith back to life, right? So sitting around feeling sad for him wasn't going to accomplish anything. It would be better if we were out there being famous and making a butt-load of money, okay? The show must go on. And what a show it turned out to be.

A show of hands indicated that everyone wanted to continue shooting. Even my hand went up. Reluctantly, but it did go up.

"Oh, one last thing," Jeremy said. "Because of the studio's concern for the safety of our cast, we're going to have twenty-four-hour security on any set and in Ian's home."

"That's a wonderful idea, Jeremy," Aurora said. "I think the cast needs to feel that this show is a safe haven, a place where they can talk about their emotions and compete in the show without being distracted. They are armed, aren't they?"

"Yes, Aurora, you are perfectly safe."

Jeremy's assistant, Tony Marcello, entered the room as

quiet as a mouse, whispered something in Jeremy's ear, then left as quickly and as silently as he entered.

"Okay, since we're all on board with continuing the show, I have an exciting new announcement to make. We have a new member on the show: Darryn Novolo. His plane just got in from New York."

The guys were even more stunned than when they found out that Keith was dead. The reason was obvious: Just when they were settling in to the idea of one less contestant, Jeremy comes in and screws it up royally.

David Laurant leaned over toward me. "Uh-ohhhhhh," he muttered.

"Bad news?" I asked.

"Just wait."

"A model?"

"Supermodel. *The* supermodel. I didn't know Ian had slept with him."

"Maybe he hasn't yet, but it could be in his plans."

Jeremy motioned for Darryn to enter the room and enter it he did. He was easily one of the most striking men I had ever seen. A perfectly elongated, slightly rounded, triangular face, with catlike green-gray eyes set perfectly far apart under deep and chiseled brows, offset the most perfectly formed pair of lips that pouted ever so slightly in the middle. His hair was slicked back in a rather rakish way. And his clothes! They were expensive, looked it, and fit like it. Probably custom tailored. No off-the-rack for this boy. It was hard to look away—you had to stare at him. You just had to. It was funny. The more you looked at him, the more he looked like a male version of the British actress Charlotte Rampling. It wasn't just the freckles that made me think of Charlotte; it was the waiflike, yet seductive innocence that dragged you in, hypnotized you. He could toy with you and not have you suspect a thing.

"Gentlemen, I'm Darryn Novolo," he said in a deep, but smooth, silky voice that just completed the picture of perfection. "Some of you are aware of me from the modeling world. I'm here to be a member of the cast, and I consider it a great honor to be allowed to be here with you on this show. And, Ian . . ." he said with the kind of sincerity lacking in this crowd and with an intonation that would make you thank him for killing your mother. "I offer my sincere condolences on the loss of your son." This guy was the definition of suave. Of refinement. He stuck out like a sore thumb in this tribe.

Darryn was going to be trouble. He was in the room for less than a minute and already it seemed that the contest was over. The guys were so disturbed by Darryn's addition to the show that they didn't seem to know what to do, how to react, or how to handle him. What disturbed me wasn't Darryn, since I didn't have a thing to lose to him, it was the fact that Jeremy added Darryn deliberately, sadistically. It's not as if the shit pot needed any more stirring. This pot was ready to boil over.

As I was musing this, another thought struck me: A few minutes ago, the future of the show was in jeopardy. So why was Darryn invited to fly across the country to be in a television program that might be canceled?

Ian commanded Drake to fetch a seat for Darryn. Drake found one and inserted it in between David and Gilles, a few people down from Ian. But Ian had other plans.

"Drake, would you be a good boy and put the chair here?" he said, pointing to a space between his chair and Gilles. The slight was glaring. Even Gilles, who was protected by inches of narcissistic armor, seemed shaken to his foundation. Darryn sat down innocent of the power play he had just been thrown into.

"So, Darryn," Ian inquired, staring through his tented fingers. "So you're *the* hottest male model in the world right now?"

Ian was up to his usual cat-and-mouse tactics.

"Thank you for the compliment, Ian, but I wouldn't say I'm the hottest male model in the world. I'm just popular right now. That could pass. I just finished several shows in Milan and four in Paris. Armani, Gucci, Prada, Dolce & Gabbana, and Versace. And here I am."

Gilles fired the first shot.

"So you are here. I see that. My question ees whyyyyyyy?" he sneered.

Darryn looked perplexed. "Because I was asked to join the cast of this show."

"But who ask you?"

"Jeremy, of course. He's the producer of this show."

"So, Darryn, he say you must come on the show, and you just come?" Gilles sniffed.

"I thought about it first, but I said yes."

"So you come on zeese program after all the hard work we have done joost to geeet your hands on Ian's money?"

Everyone waited to see if Darryn would take Gilles's toxic bait and fire back.

"I was invited to be on the show under the same circumstances that you were, Gilles."

It was an innocuous answer, but it was the right one. If it were me, I would have answered, in this order: "The only hard work you've done has involved working hard on Ian's cock." "And why, exactly, are *you* here, Gilles?" And finally,

"I think that money would be much better in my hands than yours, that way it would end up going for tasteful, stylish things and not for the disposable Eurotrash clothing and items you plow through every day." But Darryn was not going to wear his ego on his sleeve. He had good looks and he was smart. I liked him. A lot. I was slipping into my old pattern of falling for gay men.

Drake, never one to dive into battle with any of the other guys, spoke up, "Darryn, I'd like to welcome you to the show. If there's anything you need, feel free to ask me."

"Well, thank you, Drake," Darryn replied, showing 105 of the whitest teeth I had ever seen.

"So, Darryn, I'm sure that Jeremy's request that you be on the show must have come as a surprise. I've never seen you around Ian's before."

Touché, Drake. He was trying to see whose idea it was to drop Darryn as a bombshell on *Things Are a Bit Iffy*.

"I was in the middle of the Armani men's show. It was a little sudden, but I thought it would be interesting, so here I am."

I was right. Darryn was smart. Good looking. In shape. Well mannered. Just the kind of guy to win this contest. And the type to get killed. His appearance on the program affected the other guys profoundly. Aurora had pretty much ended the texting and video-game playing with a single comment. Manners were tidied up for the same reason. But it didn't take long for the guys to slip into their old routines, and the chemistry of the group, I suspect, was designed for maximum hissy fits. But Darryn changed the rules of the game in under a minute. The guys at the table were out-handsomed, out-mannered, and outsmarted. What to do? What to do?

CHAPTER 18

The Hottest Memorial Service of the Season

Funerals and memorial services. Most people dread them. The cast, however, was preparing for Keith's as a red-carpet event. Suits from Europe were arriving daily, made from previous measurements held at couturiers' headquarters in Paris, London, and Milan. Personal makeup artists swarmed Ian's house, mixing with the ones hired by the production company. And the reason for all this: This funeral was going to be filmed as part of the show. Like the carousel spinning out of control in *Strangers on a Train*, the show had taken on a life and power of its own. We had succumbed to its powers, and it made us do things we never would have considered. And we had to look good while doing it. But before you think that all I was going to do was lob stones at the others, I, too, was getting dolled up for the affair. Look at me . . . calling a memorial service an affair. I might have come under the spell of the show, but I intended to call a spade a spade.

Rows of chairs were set up in front of a raised platform with a podium on Ian's expansive grounds. There were speakers, a sound system, engineers, and banks of lighting. And all of this for us? Hardly. Yes, there were going to be all the usual luminaries from the haute couture hair world, but everyone was gearing for the possibility that Ellen De-Generes might put in an appearance as a show of support for Ian and loss of the son he didn't knew he had. While I knew Ellen was very supportive of gay causes, I felt the rumor concerning her appearance was just that—a rumor. The reality was, no one really cared about Keith, or more accurately, fewer even knew him. They were there for Ian. And the cameras. Not necessarily in that order.

Jeremy pulled us all together before attending the service and instructed us to reach down inside ourselves and try to bring up emotions.

"I want tears, sadness, empathy!"

He might as well have been asking the guys to operate a large hadron collider.

"Remember, the cameras will be on you at all times. The show's ratings are going through the ceiling, and today is another episode that is going to push it out of this world. After the memorial, we're going to assemble at a local restaurant and we're going to turn up the heat. I want to hear what you're feeling, and I want you to really let the fur fly! Okay, get out there and make this show a smash!" he said like a football coach at a deciding season game.

The cast filed out to the cameras and lights, filtering down toward the front to their reserved seats between members of the Mitchell and Sassoon hair dynasties and models, models, models. There was the shaking of hands, hugs, laughter, and to top the whole circus off, trays of drinks floated up and down the aisle propelled by waiters in tight black suits. There's nothing like liquor for throwing gasoline on the fire. There was a signal from the podium and we were all advised to take our seats by the master of ceremonies. I won't bore you with all the details of the service, but since almost no one invited knew Keith, the eulogies were centered on Ian (for his loss, presumably), which caused him to erupt in frequent outpourings of tears that ran outside his oversized and overdecorated sunglasses that engulfed most of his face. The audience was a sight to behold. The hair fashionistas sported outrageous hair styles and bad clothing while the second-tier L.A. clubbers wore sport jackets with jeans, high-top Converse sneakers, and a straw pork-pie hat—their idea of "dressing up." Everyone was busy whispering, networking, or texting.

The drone of testimonials was making me fall asleep when I was startled by a man carrying a flat wooden cage filled with a half-dozen white doves who passed down the aisle and headed for the podium. Just as it seemed that the eulogies would never end, they did. There was a lot of mumbling and fumbling; then Ian stepped up to the microphone. Ian, knowing that the cat was out of the bag, couldn't exactly relate stories of all the good times they had together. So he confined his tribute to the subject that he knew and loved best: himself. He talked about the regret of never being the dad that he should have been, which, by the time he was finished, hadn't left a dry eye in the house.

"We're now going to release doves symbolizing Keith's spirit, which we hope will soar free and up into the heavens. Fly free . . ." Ian managed to choke out through a rush of emotions, ". . . little spirit!"

A few seconds passed and the cage was raised high and the door opened. The doves, confused and startled, no doubt, by the fact that they had probably been raised in cages all their lives and were now suddenly free, flew straight up in a pack of fluttering, battering wings, bumping into each other as they struggled to find a clear direction in which to fly. What happened next, no one on earth could have foreseen.

From out of the leafy palms and eucalyptus branches came a Cooper's hawk like an F-16 fighter, hitting one of the unlucky birds in midair with such force, there was an explosion of feathers and a shower of blood that hit Ian like a well-aimed red-paint baggie thrown by a member of PETA. The hawk struggled to gain altitude with its shrieking prize in its talons and slowly it rose into the trees and disappeared. It was like watching a horrific car wreck in slow motion. This was not a good omen. Even worse, dozens of celebrity gossip stars caught the event on their smartphone movie cameras in glorious color. This little episode would be on the Internet before you could say "Mel Gibson." A few hours later when I checked the Web from the relative safety of my home office, I was proved right.

CHAPTER 19

A Memorial Luncheon to Forget

Today's shoot was a rare occasion: It was taking place at a restaurant, during which we were all there to celebrate Keith's life in a private, afternoon luncheon. Jean-Michael was the best restaurant in town, lorded over by its namesake, who moved to Palm Springs over 10 years ago and grabbed the mantel from tired, unimaginative establishments that had been resting on their dusty laurels for decades. The restaurant was closed for the rest of the day for us to film.

From the moment I walked into the restaurant, the liquor was already flowing. And so were most of the guys. From watching Aleksei's animated movements, it was obvious that he had already downed several glasses of champagne. His idea of staying clean or sober seemed to change with whatever temptation was in front of him at the time. Anything as long as it wasn't crystal meth.

There was a lot of gabbing and chatting before the cameras started rolling. You would have thought it was a black-tie fund-raiser the way everyone was so friendly and charming. Their casualness with Keith's murder was so smug, it really chapped my ass. I was going to get revenge for Keith by not letting myself be upstaged by the rest of the gang. At least that was my logic at the time. The gloves were coming off tonight. Alex was right, it was sink or swim, and I was certainly capable of swimming with the sharks.

We all sat down to eat.

Aleksei began, "Ian, I would like to offer again my condolences over the death of your son."

One camera swung quickly in Ian's direction. Ian went into the "distraught father" role for a moment, giving the camera a quick shot as he wiped a tear from his eye.

Aleksei continued, "I think it goes without saying that we are all going to miss Keith here." He poured himself another tall glass of wine right to—and over—the edge of the rim, puddling on the table below.

"Aleksei, I thought you were supposed to stop drinking?" I said, securing my place on the episode for at least a few lines.

"Hard alcohol, Amanda! Wine and beer is okay, especially if the wine is natural."

"Well, I don't mean to mother you, Aleksei, but someone here has to call you on your behavior. I don't think that rehab place you went to did you much good."

"How many times do I have to tell you, Beginnings was for chemical addiction. This is wine. It's different."

"Didn't you learn anything from their twelve-step program?"

Aleksei huffed. "They only have *four* steps. People who go there are busy people. They don't have time for all twelve. Amanda . . . let me say this, and I don't want you to take this personally: I had one mother already. I don't need another. Especially a Mommie Dearest."

"Aleksei, my suggestion is that you go find some really

good cock to suck. You can't drink with a dick in your mouth."

This comeback had the whole table whooping and clapping. I had nailed it!

While Aleksei's looks had probably gotten him everything he ever wanted (including things he never knew he wanted), they wouldn't give him a quick wit. Like I had learned in life, my intelligence occasionally came in handy. Of course, it had also led me to be saddled with four non-paying condos, a house that was never finished, and on the verge of bankruptcy, but in the meantime, I would let my wit shine and have a little fun with it.

Aleksei dropped his shield and decided not to trade blows with me right now.

As usual where food was concerned, the guys at the table picked at their food, avoiding carbs like they would the men's clothing department at Walmart . . . all except one: Marcus. He was chowing down on his appetizer and starting in on the one pushed toward him by Aleksei. He stopped chewing for a moment and got into the fray . . . in the most diplomatic way possible.

"I have to agree with what Aleksei just said"—chomp, chomp—"I think Keith was a courageous man"—chomp— "a dutiful son, and a great"—chomp—"American."

Marcus wasn't the brightest bulb in the chandelier—or the most interesting or original—but he was consistent: He never stopped brownnosing. Or showing off his muscles. I swear I'd never seen him in anything but a tank top. I'm hazarding a guess that he doesn't own a long-sleeve shirt. Then it occurred to me, there probably wasn't a dress shirt made that would fit his inflated body.

Aurora had to get in her two cents, stealing the thunder I

had established a minute ago with my great comment. "Ian . . . you don't need me to tell you how much Keith meant to all of us. And how the discovery that you had a son was a great blessing in your life that you never expected. That he was taken from us so quickly doesn't alter the fact that you now have a larger past to explore and your life has so much more meaning. I want to also say this is a wonderful menu! It's a great tribute to Keith. Basil and pink grapefruit scallops, roasted guinea hen with bay leaves, Madeira, and dates! Elderflower sorbet for dessert. This is going to be luscious, Ian. Thank you."

"It's just a shame that most of it is going to end up in a toilet thirty minutes from now," I threw in. What? It was the truth.

Usually, no one ever heard anyone else talking since they were either talking themselves or just didn't care what anyone else had to say. But it was one of those rare times when everything went suddenly dead silent, leaving my comment hanging in the clear.

David Laurant burst into a fit of laughter at my comment, clapping his hands wildly. "Boy, does she know us!"

"I take offense at that model stereotype!" Aleksei countered.

"Oh, c'mon, Aleksei. It's a wonder there's any porcelain left on your toilet bowl with all that stomach acid pouring into it. Or that you even have teeth left. What the vomit didn't take, the crystal did."

I got back in there. "I have to agree with David. You guys can do what you want in your own rooms, but there's just one bathroom for guests, and you all seem to be using it to yack up in."

Aleksei was aghast that anyone would take offense to his

purging down the hall. "Well, I don't want to use *my* toilet. It would get nasty."

"Well, thank you for being considerate of the others, Aleksei. I have to use that toilet since I am not staying here as part of the show, for your information. And additionally, if the rest of you would leave the seat down when you're finished, that would be greatly appreciated."

"Well, for your information, I do not throw up after I eat!" Aleksei snapped. "It's just that sometimes my stomach is a little unsettled."

"Ho-boy," Gilles said, giving the hornet's nest a good kick. "Considering za amount of zperm you swallow, it is no wonder your stomach, she is upset."

Marcus laughed. "He's had more cum in him than a donor freezer at a sperm bank."

"Well, at least I don't drink pee!" Aleksei countered.

"I don't drink pee! That's Gatorade I have in my hydration bottle at the gym."

"Not all the time," Drake added.

"I need to keep my electrolytes up. Whoever started that rumor, I wish they would stop. I've never done that, have I, Ian?" Marcus pleaded, hoping to draw Ian into a hasty defense.

"Marcus, you know I never hiss and tell. Well, hardly."

"Well," David chimed in, "I seem to remember a certain muscular guy running around Jake Harrington's New Year's Eve party in L.A. wearing a diaper and peeing in it."

Marcus's face got so red, I thought it was going to pop. Of course, it usually looked like that from the steroids he took to maintain his knockwurst body. So to be accurate, he went from shiny red to more of a blood orange. Stand back. I think he's going to blow.

"Well, since we're on the subject of alternative sexual tastes, David, I guess you had a good view of me from the top of your platform stiletto black vinyl boots. And the latex corset/bustier combo. It *is* enforced feminization you're into, isn't it, *Daisy?*"

David was aghast. "You said you would never tell!"

"I said I would never mention the pony stuff either. But I guess it's all the same thing: You're always wearing tall heels."

While I tried to figure out what *pony stuff* was, David puffed himself up and lobbed a Molotov cocktail back at Marcus.

"Well, when you're sitting in an adult-sized baby crib and sucking on a pacifier, you don't have time for shoes. Unless they're baby shoes."

Drake, usually the model for restraint until Darryn came along, tried to douse the flames that seemed to be breaking into a full-fledged wildfire.

"Guys, guys, could we keep this civilized?"

"Oh yeah, Drake . . ." Aleksei sputtered, preparing to fire on all cylinders. "You should talk, Mister Dominator . . . beat 'em up for money! Money!" Aleksei laughed. "You welted Ian's azz so badly, he couldn't sit down for a billlllion yearssssss!"

Drake shot one of his bird-of-prey glances, which for the first time failed to intimidate the guys around the table. Maybe it was because we had an audience of millions of people worldwide for protection? I mean, now that we knew that Drake was a professional dominant, he wasn't going to leap up and beat Aleksei to a pulp. Was he?

So that explains Drake's smoldering, dangerous look, I thought to myself.

"But, Drake, Drake, Dra . . ." Aleksei continued slurring. "I love you. Love you . . . love the way you strangle me un-tillll I cummmmm."

From BDSM to autoeroticism, Drake was a busier guy than I thought. So was everyone in the house, for that matter. The whole cast seemed to be involved in a hotbed of sexual interludes, all going on without me so much as suspecting more than a little hide the salami. I felt like a dumb prude.

I pushed my chair back from the table a few inches just in case I needed to make a hasty retreat. Aleksei quickly poured himself another glass of wine and downed it like it was the last one on earth. Ian, instead of being equally embarrassed, seemed to enjoy the shock value his prurient tastes were going to give the world when the details were released. I guess if you wanted to be remembered, you wanted to go out with a bloody great bang. People rarely remember the polite and unassuming.

Aleksei continued his scorched-earth policy and finally turned on the one person who had ribbed him so long and hard: Gilles. Aleksei was quickly getting quite drunk, so his insult was not going to be all that witty, but a punch in the mouth was a punch in the mouth.

"And you, Mister . . . French fry. Gilles," he said, pronouncing the silent "s" at the end of his name. "Gilles who squeals during sex. Like a pig. That rubber pig mask he wears during sex! That izzz too funnnny! Oink, oink, Gilles!"

Gilles got up from the table in a huff and headed in the direction of the sideboard to pour himself another tall glass of tomato juice.

Lance Greenly, who was standing behind the sidelines

watching the luncheon being filmed, suddenly spoke up—a rare occurrence since he almost never talked. And talk he did. Or he raised his voice a little beyond his usual squeak. And shook as he talked, he was so angry.

"You're all a bunch of nitwits! Empty-headed nitwits! Here, Ian supports you and gives you more money than you deserve, and still it's never enough. It just turns my stomach to think of the money you've taken and never said thanks to Ian. And now here you are, trying to get your hands on even more! Disgusting!" he finished, then walked away.

Everyone was speechless for a millisecond, then resumed whatever they were doing. My cell phone rang, causing me to scramble to get it out of my purse and fumble to turn it off.

"I thought we made an announ-ze-ment," Aleksei said, slurring his speech, "that we were to turn our fuckin' zellphones off before we started filming. I guezz that applies to everyone except beards!" he finished, laughing at his own joke, even though it was a private joke.

Darryn got up from the table to get more food at the buffet on the sideboard. And to get away from the toxic atmosphere at the table.

I finally got my cell phone out as it continued to ring and vibrate in my hand like a cicada on too much caffeine. I got my finger into the On/Off switch and promptly broke a nail in a jagged—and painful—rip halfway down to my cuticle. "Ow!" I shouted, and shook my hand to relieve the pain. "Okay, it's off!" I almost shouted back.

Exactly four seconds later, my phone rang again. I thought I had turned it off, but I guess I didn't push the slider Silence button completely off. I tried again, but with my broken nail, it wasn't easy. Or painless. Success at last. I threw the phone down on the table.

"And I wuh like to say somesin to Auror . . . a. . . . roar-ah now," Aleksei said, the slurs insinuating their way into more words. He threw back another glass of wine, missing most of his mouth and saturating his shirt collar.

My cellphone came to life again, vibrating on the tabletop, which amplified the buzzing tenfold as it danced around, doing the hokeypokey. Aleksei, ready to lock his targeting mechanism onto anything that moved or left a heat signature, fired away at me.

"Ar-man-dah," he managed to get out. "I know you have sexual needzzz like the rest of uz, but please get your ga-damn vibrator off the table and keep it in the drawer in your ni . . . stand," he said, laughing.

I was shocked at how fast the wine was going to his head. He was getting insanely drunk by the second.

"So where was I?" he asked, giggling at forgetting his train of thought, which was currently derailed. A train wreck, to be more accurate. "Oh, yeah, Au . . . Au. . . . Wowah!" More giggling. "Wait, I forgot," he said, falling blessedly silent.

Marcus tried to wrestle the conversation back to something more inert. "Well, wonderful meal, Ian. I guess we'll have to think of something to do to work this meal off," he said with a lascivious smile at Ian.

"Yes, it is," Darryn said from a safe distance as he spooned some tomatoes onto his plate. "I mean, a wonderful meal, that is." He finished, then again took his place next to me.

My phone buzzed again. I looked around and challenged everyone within eyesight to call me on it. *Just try me*, my

151

eyes blazed. Someone was desperately trying to reach me. Alex, calling to tell me Knucklehead had inadvertently set the house on fire? One of my listings had a gas leak and exploded, leveling the Vista Las Palmas neighborhood? I looked at the phone and it was an MMS multimedia message of a guy's asshole. Yes, someone had sent me a picture of their asshole. I looked at the sender and surprise! It was none other than my asshole client (pun intended) Vicktor Teller. The message under his unbleached anus:

You can kiss this good-bye, bitch. I'll get someone else to sell my house!!!!

I was three inches from completely snapping. You read about housewives taking all they can, calmly hitting their husbands with a frying pan, then sitting down to watch the afternoon soaps. I was just about to go there.

The storm had not yet passed, however. Aleksei roared back to life again. Taking off in yet another direction.

"Oh, I got a piece of gossip. Hot, hot, hot, hot, hot . . . sizzin' hot fuggin hot. Hot. You ne'er guess who I zaw kissing here in the house! I was shocked. No, diz-gust-ted," he said, sticking his finger down his throat in a mock vomiting gesture.

Unfortunately, Aleksei's motor skills were sorely lacking and he went a little too far down the pipe, erupting in a shower of vomit that spewed out of his mouth in a Niagara of wine and . . . other things I don't care to mention, or identify. Unfortunately, Aleksei had some motor skills left: He hit me squarely from across the table with pinpoint accuracy.

"THAT'S IT!" I shrieked like a banshee, composing

myself only to the point of being able to force words out through my clenched teeth. "I am so sick of all this horseshit! I can't take it anymore. I agree with Lance. I'm sick of the way you guys are sucking up to Ian for his money when most of you couldn't care less about him! All this bitching and moaning, and your eating disorders, your enemas to avoid going to the toilet like poorer people, and going on and on about stuff that's so stupid and shallow, it wouldn't even make it into the dialogue of a Quentin Tarantino movie! Bleaching your assholes, plucking your pubes, and now, I learn, acting like babies with pacifiers, cross-dressing, wearing pig masks, and getting spanked so you can't even sit on your lily-white assholes!"

Aurora tried to intervene by reaching up and putting a hand on my shoulder, but I wasn't finished.

"I'm not finished with all of you yet . . ." I continued, as David and Marcus tried to leave the room. ". . . and that means you too. I've listened to all of you for long enough, so now you can stand here until I've said what I need to say. I have had it up to here with everything"—I held my level hand to my forehead, then lowered it to my navel and looked straight at Marcus—"and I've had it up to here with you! So you're short and your balls have shrunk to the size of marbles because you're juicing all the time to make up for the fact that you're short. So what! The other guys make fun of you! Boo hoo. People say I look like someone punched Kathleen Turner in the nose. So what?!"

Several of the guys muttered that they finally figured out whom I reminded them of.

"Since we're making the rounds, David, I like you, but you've got the empathy of an Auschwitz commandant, and you need to find *one* personality with *one* look and stick to it.

Gilles, you have an amazing butt and a huge cock, and that's about it. You have none of the wit, the charm, or the sophistication of the people of Paris. I said it at the beginning and I still stand by my original proclamation: You're just cheap, gold-digging Eurotrash. Drake, you're another one I'm disappointed in. You're smart, handsome, and yet you run around Ian's estate picking up the shit his dogs leave all over the yard. And now I learn you perhaps earn your keep by beating up Ian. I as much as any of you would like to beat up Ian, but, Drake, you're wasting your life being stuck here because Ian pays you for it. Go out, get a real job. Yeah, it might not pay as much, but at least you won't have to put up with anyone else's shit. Darryn? You I like. You're perfect. Now for Ian. I can't believe that a man who created this huge empire can be so petty. You have guys followed, you pit the guys against each other, and you don't seem to care that you had sex with your son. You need to grow up . . . and go get a haircut . . . I hate that ponytail! And to Mrs. Gorky, my client with her overpriced house in Vista Las Palmas," I said, looking directly at a camera that was capturing me. "Your house is a dump. D-U-M-P! It's way overpriced! It has the curb appeal of a sewage-pumping station, it smells like Coney Island at low tide inside because you won't stop cooking sardines for breakfast, and you look like you hired Marilyn Manson to do your makeup. And to my ex-client Vicktor Teller, you're an asshole, and here's the photo of yours that you just sent me," I said, holding the photo on my iPhone to the camera. "Very classy. With all those wide-screen TVs out there, viewers might just be able to take your whole ass in!"

"Well, Amanda . . ." Aurora tried to cut in.

"Wait! I'm not finished! And what's the thing with fitted

sheets! How the hell are you supposed to fold the god-damned things until you're ready to use them? And last, but not least, why am I supposed to care about Lindsay Lohan or Paris Hilton? I really don't care!"

"Thank you, Amanda, for that wonderful mental melt-down with a touch of Seinfeld near the end," Aurora inter-jected. "I hope you had a good catharsis."

As Aurora tried to move things along, no one else moved a muscle for what seemed the longest time. No one spoke. Anyone who was still standing near me had a trapped look on their face and slowly made their way out of the room, as did the rest, slowly trickling away.

"Since we were on the subject of assholes a minute ago, this one"—I pointed at Aleksei, who had passed out—"needs to be put into a car, driven home, and put to bed. If I could get a little help from one of you guys," I pleaded, but the men in the room were holding their hands over their noses and turning their heads away in disgust.

"He's covered with vomit. Eewww!" David exclaimed in disgust. "I'm not touching him. Maybe if you let him sit in his own vomit, that will teach him a lesson."

"I'll do it!" I said. "You guys are all supposed to be such icons of masculinity, but you're all a bunch of big pussies," I said, getting up and wiping Aleksei off with several nap-kins. "You get the legs, and I'll get him behind his shoul-ders," I instructed Aurora.

Despite the fact that Aleksei was exactly six feet one inch tall, he weighed close to nothing since he was a model who found eating a necessary evil in life. I also took several outdoor survival classes with Alex and learned how to carry a wounded hiking partner if necessary.

Aurora and I carried Aleksei out to *my* car, whereupon I

drove him home, with Aurora and Darryn gallantly volunteering to help me carry him upstairs and down the long hall to his room. Aurora suggested that we leave him seated in a wing chair.

"Why's that?" I asked.

"From the look of the table downstairs, I think he's purged just about everything in him . . ." Aurora said.

"You mean entire Mondavi vineyards?"

"Yes, but there's no guarantee he doesn't have more coming. I say we leave him upright. I'm afraid if he sleeps on his back or side, he runs the risk of choking on his vomit."

"One Jimi Hendrix is enough," I agreed. We took his shirt and pants off, and left him sitting comfortably in his chair, putting a bucket from a nearby bathroom in his lap, just in case, and closed the door. We started down the hall, when I grabbed Aurora's arm and stopped her.

"What?" Aurora asked.

"I'm not sure I can go down there."

"Because you gave them all a much-needed kick in the groin? Honey, if I worried about what everyone thought about what I said, I wouldn't be where I am today."

"And where is that?" I asked.

"Splattered in vomit, but a rising star in the field of relationship counseling."

CHAPTER 20

Amanda Thorne, Incorporated

My filming schedule had become too much for me to take care of my real-estate business, so I turned everything over to Alex. My rising stardom was lassoing clients in right and left, and Alex took on the extra work himself with his usual otherworldly ability to handle a hundred things at once.

I stopped at his house and was signing some paperwork when he looked up at me and asked, "Do you have a publicist? I got a call from a Naomi Ballington wanting to know if you'd seen the Web site yet."

"Well, yes, Alex. I'm having someone handle my publicity. I've got a blog, Twitter account, and a possible upcoming book deal."

"A book? About your experiences on the show?"

"No, not yet. This is a how-to."

"How to get on the show?"

"No, a You-Know-You're-a-Fag-Hag-When . . . book."

"You've got to be joking!"

"I am not, Alex. My publisher thinks it will be a big seller. Think of the all the straight women who married gay men. Constance Lloyd to Oscar Wilde. Linda Lee Thomas married to Cole Porter. Liza to Peter Allen. Frida Kahlo to Diego Rivera."

"Diego was straight. It was Frida who had affairs with women."

"Okay, but you get my point. Maybe Fran Drescher will buy a copy."

"So when did this publicity machine crank up? I didn't even know you were working with a P.R. firm."

"An agent, actually. Vanessa Plant. Naomi is my Web site strategist."

"You have an agent? This is shocking. You never mentioned it to me."

"It happened just a week ago."

"So how did you find this agent?"

"She found me, Alex. That's why I went with her. She's on top of things. A real shark. You gotta have an agent like that nowadays. Someone who wants to win. Aren't you glad that I'm making all these changes in my life? Being assertive. Taking what's mine."

"Wow, I had no idea you had all these deals going on."

"They're not all definite, but my agent is working on them. Oh, and I've got a few product endorsements in the works."

"Product endorsements?"

"You remember when I had the wardrobe malfunction with Gilles?"

"Booby Nights?"

"Yes, it turns out that several companies that make breast enhancement exercise devices want me to endorse some of their products. I could be the celebrity spokesperson for the BusterAll. It's a bust-enlarging secret from Lithuania, heavily guarded for centuries and now used by the hottest fashion models from Lithuania."

"I didn't realize that your grandmother's homeland was such a hotbed of fashionistas."

"It is now. At least that's what the advertising manager for this bust thing said. I'm not going too far with this stuff, am I?"

Alex hesitated for probably a nanosecond before he responded—something that would have gone unnoticed by anyone else, but to me it was like getting slapped across the face. "Uh, sure. It's great. Milk it for all it's worth. Make hay while the sun shines."

I got it. The disappointment . . . a look I was used to all my life. From my parents. The nuns. From teachers. Countless dates. I could have found the cure for cancer, but all it took was one look from a disapproving scientist and I would have thrown the life-saving formula into the trash. I didn't say a thing to Alex, but we were still soul mates: I could read his mind and he mine. A few words with just the right, but almost imperceptible, inflection spoke volumes to the other. He had telegraphed his concern to me about the direction my life was taking and I got the message loud and clear. But would I listen to it? That was the $64,000 question.

"Thanks, Alex. Thanks," was all I could say.

CHAPTER 21

I Now Pronounce You Empress Dowager

When I took Knucklehead to the Bark Park behind city hall to see his dog friends and chase a tennis ball ceaselessly, people gathered around me. Celebrity was infectious. People who hadn't seen *Things Are a Bit Iffy* on television or the Internet had been told by friends to watch it, or sent e-mails with links in them. It wasn't just during the day either that I was really getting attention. On the Internet, hundreds of men seemed to have gotten hold of my e-mail address and flooded my mailbox with everything from well wishes to disgusting and gross proposals involving everything from watching me wrestle another woman in a pen of whipped cream to eating sushi off my body and vomit sex. On top of that, I started going out to the bars every night with Regina in tow. And on those nights when Regina's seemingly endless energy level began to ebb—or I didn't want her to cockblock me—I went out by myself, with gay men flocking around me when I went to gay bars and straight men circling when I hit the straight ones. And the men really started hitting on me. Men who had never given me a glance before were now trying to pick me up. Or marry me. One night, a businessman from Taiwan asked me to marry him, come back to Taiwan, and live like a Tai Tai—a privileged lady of means who spends her time lunching and indulging herself while the husband works himself to death to support the Tai Tai. It sounded like a good plan to me. He said he made over $4 million last year (I asked him, "In U.S. dollars?!"), not including bonuses, and I didn't doubt it when I said good-bye to him at a Mercedes SLS that must have set him back hundreds of thousands of dollars. Believe me, being underwater and in debt with four nonperforming condos, a mortgage on my main house, and credit cards maxed out, I gave this proposal a lot of thought. A lot. But in the end, I turned the guy down. After all, I didn't speak Mandarin, was repulsed by the idea of raw clams (soaked in *any* sauce), and felt I would get stir-crazy living on such a small island. Of course, I could fly over to Hong Kong to go shopping or Macao for gambling, but Taiwan was just too uncertain to me. What I was sure of was that my constant barhopping to give my ego a boost was really kicking my ass and body when it all came down to it. I looked in the mirror, and I was looking haggard, worn-out, and old. If it's true that television cameras put ten pounds on you, I feared what it did when it came to years.

CHAPTER 22

Here, Let Me Help You Tie Your Tie

Another day of shooting. There were still weeks and weeks of shooting to go. It was exhausting, starting at the crack of dawn and working until late in the evening at times. I had a newfound appreciation for television stars.

As usual, we were sitting in Iffy Central, Ian's cavernous living room where the bulk of the scenes from the show were filmed. We were made up, meticulously but casually dressed, and ready to go. With one small change in the scene to be shot. Darryn's presence on the show had caused all the others to "lose their edge," as Jeremy stated. With the exception of the welcomed debacle of the memorial luncheon the day before, Jeremy was getting pissed off that the drama was ebbing out of the show. He needed more drama, more catfighting, he stressed. He wanted to keep the ratings on their rocket trajectory.

"Jeremy," David stated. "You want us to be dramatic, but we end up suffering for it since Aurora is grading us on our behavior. This is putting us between a rock and a hard place."

"The only hard place you have been lately has been Ian's bedroom," Gilles snapped.

"There!" Jeremy exclaimed. "That's the toxic behavior I remember. I want more of that—just wittier lines than that. Okay, guys, let's get started."

The cameramen got into position and started. Lights, action, attitude!

"David," Ian started. Could you go upstairs and see what's keeping Aleksei?"

"Ian!" he complained. "Every time I go to fetch someone, they end up dead. I'm not doing this again," he said, putting down his Diet Coke on a priceless end table without a coaster. He got up and plodded upstairs like he had a 1,000-pound weight on his shoulders.

The moment this observation slipped from David's mouth, you could see that everyone was thinking the same thing: something bad has happened to Aleksei. You saw the concerned faces shooting glances at each other to see if they were thinking the same thing. You saw hands tapping on chair armrests. A nervous cough or two.

"It's weird. I haven't seen Aleksei all morning," Drake mentioned. "I at least get treated to hearing him vomiting before he goes to bed at night, then in the morning after he has a yogurt, coffee, and a cigarette."

"Breakfast of Champions," I added. It was a good line, but it had none of the zing of some of my earlier precision strikes. I was getting tired. My lines were getting tired, too, I feared.

Presently, David came back downstairs and flopped himself on the couch, picking up his Diet Coke and fashion magazine.

"Well?" Drake asked.

"Well what?" David replied, clearly not understanding that the mood had shifted tectonically in his absence.

"What did you find out?" Drake asked.

"Oh, there's a loose tile in the hallway outside my room. I nearly tripped on it for the second time. Ian, could you get Drake to get that fixed? Someone's going to get really hurt on that tile."

Drake leaned forward in his armchair and said through gritted teeth, "David, is Aleksei joining us?"

"Aleksei? Joining us? Probably not."

"Could you tell us why?" Drake continued.

"He's sitting upstairs with a tie twisted around his neck. A striped rep tie. Can you imagine? I mean, it's 2012! Like some kinda fuckin' Ralph Lauren preppie tie thing . . . sorry, Drake. I know how you like Ralphie, having worked for him a long time ago. Hey, maybe it's one of your ties!"

"How would you know it's one of my ties?"

"No one else would wear a rep tie around here but you, Drake."

Drake and the rest of us went upstairs in what was becoming a regular routine.

"Well, don't get mad at me, Drake! I hear rep ties are making a comeback for spring!" David added before we were out of earshot.

We gathered at Aleksei's door like a weary band of tourists, staring but not registering what we were seeing. There in a wing chair with its back to us was Aleksei, sitting naked and upright with a tie twisted tightly around his neck, his face a purple–blue. Since we were all tall, we could see over the top of the back of the chair—all except Marcus, who leaned far into the room to get a good look, holding on to the door molding with veiny, muscular hands.

"Careful, Marcus," I intoned. "We can't disturb evidence."

"I won't step into the room. I've hung on a cross bar like

this for forty minutes before," Marcus said proudly. "Shit," he said, staring at Aleksei.

Darryn, who stood at the back of the pack, whispered, "This is really freaky. Aren't you scared?"

"With all these people around, no. Plus, they're not after me. They're after you guys."

"Thanks a lot. You've made me feel a whole lot better," Darryn replied. "I am not sleeping in this house."

Just then, a voice spoke up from behind all of us. "Now, if you skyscrapers would step out of the way, a short person would like to get a look-see," Aurora said.

The boys parted for Aurora, who stood in the doorway.

"Jesus Christ! Who is doing this?" she asked, shaking her head. "Wait a minute. . . . Hey, look over there on the dresser. Drugs!"

She was right. From my vantage point, I could see the pile of whitish crystals on the top of Aleksei's tall dresser.

Aurora continued, "It looks like autoerotic asphyxiation. He snorted some crystal, wanted to jerk off because he was on a high, and he got the tie too tight and fainted before he passed out. I have a lot of male patients who are into it. But I can't tell you who. Patient–therapist confidentiality."

I decided to play detective.

"It seems coincidental, people. We have one murder, and now another person just happens to die in the house, but this time it's self-induced? It's all too coincidental. No, this is another murder."

"I don't know, Amanda," Drake said. "Look at the floor in front of Aleksei. He's sprayed his chowder all over the place. He was cumming just as he passed out from the tie. Happens all the time."

I looked around to be certain there was a camera on me; there was.

"My question is," I said like a great detective, "where Aleksei got the tie. He doesn't strike me as the kind of guy who would wear a tie, especially a rep tie. As David said downstairs, those are the kinds of ties that you wear, Drake. Would you care to shed a little light on this development?"

David joined our little group of survivors. He brightened up when he looked at Aleksei again. "I saw an episode of *Six Feet Under* where a guy was doing the same thing, but you're supposed to suck on a lemon, so if you start to pass out from the lack of oxygen to the brain, you bite down on the lemon and the shock of the tartness wakes you up before you strangle yourself."

David's theory sounded plausible . . . if it had come from someone else.

"All we need to do is look around and see if there's a lemon wedge somewhere in the room. Mystery solved," David said.

"No one is going anywhere into the room."

"Or," David said casually, "Drake was strangling Aleksei erotically and things got out of hand."

Dead silence. Drake, who normally could frighten the others with a looks-that-could-kill sideways glance, looked more like a trapped animal.

David attempted to enter the room again as I grabbed him by the shoulder and restrained him.

"We've got to keep the place clear," I said sternly.

"Zo who makes you the Hercule Poirot?" Gilles from behind.

"Nobody, but it's just good police procedure," I added.

"You zeem to know a lot about ze police," Gilles continued. "Maybe you know a lot about murder also. Keeling people!" he said, making a slashing motion with his hand holding an imaginary knife.

"Gilles, as usual, you are being overly dramatic."

"You . . ." he said, pointing at me with his perfect finger. "You, I get zee restraining order on you. You slap me, now you want to murder me."

"Gilles, if you're talking about the number of people waiting to murder you, the line starts somewhere back near the Louvre."

Finally, a great zinger of a response and the cameramen got it. I was back on top. Since Jerry warned them not to photograph crime scenes or even approach them, the cameramen stayed their distance. But a zoom lens solved that problem. I only worried that because this scene might compromise a murder investigation, the police might not allow it to air. As they say in the theater, the best scene might end up being played off stage.

The security guards that were hired to protect us finally showed up with bags of hamburgers and fries in their hands. By that time, the police had arrived again, setting up shop with regularity that was almost wearying. Another day, another murder. Everyone had been shooed downstairs. Jerry arrived and escorted me upstairs with him.

"Upstairs she go again, the murderess," Gilles sniped.

Before I got out of eyesight, I turned around for the cameras and stuck out my tongue at Gilles. We headed to Aleksei's room where Jerry surveyed the scene before going in.

"Everyone seems to think this was unintentional suicide, Jerry."

"Suicide? Who thinks that?"

"Everyone. Even Aurora."

"Oh, in that case, I can just pack up and go home now. A celebrity shrink thinks it was suicide."

"So you don't think so?" I asked as Jerry made his way carefully into the room.

"No, I *know* so. Look at the way the tie has been pulled up from behind . . . er, Adam's . . . ?"

"Aleksei's."

". . . Aleksei's neck. See the marks on the neck? The abrasions are at the back, with most of them pointing vertically. The tie was pulled way up. In fact, you can see from the marks on the chair's velvet upholstery, on the arms, that Aleksei was pulled up and struggled with his hands, pushing down to take the tension off his neck. Whoever did this was very tall."

"That eliminates one person downstairs: Marcus Blade."

"Mini-Me Hulk downstairs?"

"He can't be five foot two. Then there's Aurora, she's short too."

"So everyone else is tall?" Jerry asked.

"Everyone. Even Ian and me. Well, Lance Greenly, Ian's CEO, is about five foot eight."

"So I assume the pile of drugs here on the dresser is crystal meth?"

"Probably. Aleksei had a problem with it and was here recuperating from it."

Jerry pulled a folding magnifying glass from his back pocket.

"That is soooo Sherlock Holmes," I said.

"Elementary, my dear Amanda."

He bent over Aleksei and looked closely up his nose.

"Trying to see if he snorted any crystal?"

"Yes. Good girl. Yup, there's some up his nostril, but the medical examiner will tell us if it goes all the way up."

"Why would it not go all the way up into his nasal passages?"

"Just a hunch, Amanda. Just a hunch."

"Are there other ways of doing crystal, Jerry?"

"Smoking it. But I don't see a pipe anywhere."

"He could have put it away in a drawer, or hidden it," I suggested.

"If he was deliberately going to get high here in his room—and you said he was an addict—then he knew he would be high for a long time."

"So what does that have to do with the price of tea in China?" I asked.

"What's the rush in putting a pipe away? Or a needle if he was injecting? There's plenty of time to put things away. Plus, you never know. Meth is so addictive, the user always knows he's going to want more eventually."

"So those are the only ways of getting high on meth?"

"Some use it as an anal suppository, Amanda."

"Oh?"

"I'm not checking there, if that's what you're driving at. But be my guest."

"No thanks, Jerry. So you don't think he was high and jerking off doing a little autoerotic asphyxiation?"

Jerry looked at me with all seriousness. "This is not to leave this room."

I made a sign of crossing my heart.

"No, he might have been jerking off, but I doubt the autoerotic part."

"Do you think the killer jerked him off after he died?

Isn't that possible? I heard that men can have erections after being hanged."

Jerry looked at me like I was crazy. "You think someone got him sexually aroused after he was strangled?"

Maybe I was crazy. "No," I said. "I guess not. I have trouble getting guys aroused when they're completely awake and alive."

"You? I can't imagine it. A sexy woman like you?"

Normally, I would have deflected his compliment and crushed it with a joke, but this time I didn't. The look in Jerry's eyes stopped me in my tracks. His eyes were mischievous, teasing, tempting. The look lasted for only a second, but it was there nonetheless. I was being hit on. It stunned me. I wasn't prepared. But then again, how does one prepare for something like this?

"Jerry, I don't know what to say."

"Maybe it's best if you didn't say anything," he replied, looking around the room for perhaps a diversion? "Anyway . . ."

"Yes . . ." I said, like an adulterous wife who narrowly escaped getting caught cheating. And just like that, we went back to our old lives. Respectable. Professional. Uninvolved. Not starting an affair.

"How about a DNA sample?" Jerry asked.

"Excuse me, I'm not that kind of girl."

"No, Amanda, I'm going to have the crime people take a DNA sample of the sperm here on the floor. I'm suspicious . . . Just a hunch."

"You have a lot of hunches, Jerry."

"That's all my job is, Amanda. Hunches that need to be proved correct."

"You know, Jerry, I have a few myself. I guess I need to check them out. What I don't understand is why someone . . . wait a minute! Aleksei really shot his mouth off yesterday at Jean-Michael's. He probably said something he shouldn't have."

"And I assume it was all on film?"

"On tape, if you want to be technical. High-definition videotape. Call it what you want."

"I think we need to look at that footage as soon as possible. Our answer to this whole mess might just be on there."

CHAPTER 23

What A Load of Fertilizer

Later that afternoon, I decided to go looking for answers myself. First stop: the potting shed in the backyard. I left Ian's house and walked the expansive lawn toward the back of the eight-car garage. As I neared the shed, I could have sworn someone was there walking behind me. I stopped and turned around quickly but saw no one. Were all these murders creeping me out? Was my mind playing tricks on me?

I entered the unlocked shed and stood there silently, taking it all in. What was I looking for? I wish I knew. Maybe I'd see something that might spur my mind if I saw it. If I were Hercule Poirot, I would start by thinking about what might have happened; then I would reconstruct the steps of the crime. Okay, I didn't have a French accent, but I could live with that. Everything had been gone over by the police and was back in its proper place, so I was looking at everything that was there the day of the murder. If what I was looking for was there in the first place. One thing at a time.

I looked at everything in the shed and went through the inventory, item by item, taking them down and examining them, then putting them back exactly where I got them.

On the top shelf was the gopher poison and a bottle of Malathion. Spotless bottles of poison. Agatha Christie would have loved this. The next shelf down, Miracle-Gro, bone-meal, and two labeled wooden boxes, one containing three pairs of gardening gloves, the other containing three garden trowels. Again, spotless. The gloves looking like they had never touched dirt. Mine, I had to admit, were never this clean. No dirt on them whatsoever. Drake apparently washed them after every use. Just two shelves. On the main potting table, there were just four pots, all containing succulents presumably ready to go out in the yard now that the days were slowly getting cooler. Also, there was a small, four-drawer cabinet filled with twist ties and a pad of paper with a list of more plants under the heading "To Buy." I looked at the pad to see if there were impressions on the pages below made by previous notes, but nothing was discernible. Under the table on a shelf below was a dented half-gallon paint can to hold paint while painting, two two-gallon paint cans of latex Ralph Lauren paint (I shook them just to make sure there was paint in them), a jar of eight different paintbrushes all so clean you'd think they were never dipped in paint, and finally, toward the back, an opened bag of bonemeal. I hauled the heavy bag to the front, took the five perfectly spaced clothespins off the top, and stuck my hand inside, looking for a gun or something dangerous. I felt plastic toward the bottom, grabbed at it, and pulled out a . . . a baggie with hundreds of dollars in it. Followed by another. And another. And another. No, not hundreds. Thousands. I counted one bag and estimated the amount in the others and came up with a figure of $87,000. Had the cops missed all this? In the bottom of the fifth baggie, there was a key that looked like a safe deposit key. (I know, since I carried one on my key ring.) I put the baggies back, burying them down at the bottom of the bag. On the floor . . . I just couldn't get over the money. Eighty-seven thousand! And probably much more than that in a safety deposit box in a bank somewhere, all of it, no doubt, belonging to Drake. I imagined Drake was planning his escape from Casa de Ian. Or he was embezzling from Ian, skimming money off the top of his estate. Anyway, not my business. Okay, back to work. On the floor, I pulled out three pots filled with gravel, sand, and the last one, Japanese river rocks. All white. I explored deep inside the pots but came up with nothing.

And those were the contents of the shed. Not much to go on, unless you thought that keeping close to $100,000 in a bag of bonemeal was suspicious. I exited the shed and closed the door behind me. I still swear someone was watching me, eyes peering from somewhere unknown, but after scanning the ficus hedges, the Mediterranean fan palm groves, and the visible upper stories of the various windows that looked down on this part of the yard, I concluded that it was just the heebie-jeebies caused by the fact that a murderer was still stalking around, maybe waiting to strike again. It was natural to feel this way, I told myself.

CHAPTER 24

Maybe You Should Talk To A Psychiatrist About That

Since I was on a roll, I felt like I needed to talk with someone who wasn't an obvious suspect. That ruled out the entire crew, Ian, Jeremy, and his assistant, Tony. Even though Darryn wasn't even in town when Keith was bumped off, I ruled him out as too much of an outsider and not in the know about what was going on at Ian's estate. I sat down next to Aurora, itching to get started. If anyone could shed some light on this whole mess, it would be her.

I wanted to meet Aurora on neutral territory, so we met at a dark Mexican restaurant that no one ever went to. I didn't want anyone from the cast coming in and seeing me with Aurora. A lot of the guys in the tribe weren't too smart, but they would know enough if they walked in and saw me talking to Aurora.

Aurora stilted into the restaurant on towering heels, dressed in her usual black. (I wondered what she would look like in pastels.). She sat down and folded her long hands on the table in front of me, her black nails clacking loudly before they came to a silent rest.

"So what was so urgent and secret that you had to meet

me here . . . and that I couldn't tell anyone about?" she asked.

I leaned forward, not to keep my conversation volume low, but because I was becoming quite the actress. I wanted to add some drama.

"I want you to tell me everything you know about everyone."

"Amanda!" Aurora replied incredulously. "That would take forever. Plus, remember, what I know about Ian is held in the strictest confidence."

"But you can tell me about the rest of the cast, can't you? And Jeremy and Tony and Lance?"

"Of course. I'm not treating them."

"Great! Let's start with the non-cast members."

"Amanda, you're trying to figure out who killed Keith, aren't you? You didn't invite me here because you want to get something over the other cast members, did you?"

"Aurora, I have nothing to gain by learning the other guys' dirty secrets . . . but wait . . . have other guys from the show approached you for that purpose?"

"All of them! Look, we all know these guys aren't going to write a discourse on the meaning of the Arab Spring to Western democracies, but they know how to defend their turf and play dirty and fight back when they need to."

"So let's start. Jeremy and his little sycophant, what's-his-name? How did you get to know him?"

"What do you mean, Amanda?"

"I mean that you obviously had to know him somehow. How did he come up with the idea for the show?"

Aurora thought for a moment. "I think he knew Ian somehow. Or maybe he went to Ian to get his hair styled. I can't remember exactly. Do you want their entire history, or just how you think they might be involved in Keith's murder?"

"Through the filter of your psychological insight."

"This won't go outside this room?"

"You have my word, Aurora."

"Okay. Do I think Jeremy could have killed Keith? For ratings? Sure. He's driven, maniacal. Plus, he's a producer. They're bloodthirsty people who are only as good as their last movie or series. The money is part of it, but it's really the ego that has to be fed. They live in L.A., so they're constantly surrounded by stars, agents, studio execs . . . all of whom they think are judging them. And, to be honest, they *are* being judged. In Hollywood, the reality is a big, paranoid, cultish, collective bunch that is so skewed from the rest of the planet. Jeremy's is a slowly rising star. He's had some real failures, so those are still chasing him. But he's had a few mild successes, which no one remembers. But this show? Whew. He knows that Keith's murder is going to shoot this show into the heavens. I mean, even before the murder, the premise was outrageous: A dying multimillionaire who's going to give away a lot of his fortune to a guy based on a contest? It blows *American Idol* and *America's Got Talent* completely away. Now we've got a murdered contestant. You'd have to be insane not to want to watch something like this. Plus, he has an assistant."

"What do you mean by that?"

"It's easier to carry out a murder if you don't have to do it all by yourself. Two are easier than one."

"Two are also more likely to leave clues. Twice as many mistakes to make."

"Interesting observation, Amanda. Next?"

"Let's go through the cast. Let's start with Drake."

"Okay. Drake's smart. Reserved."

"A leather dominant," I said.

"Yes, he is. Ian likes to be dominated by him."

"That's so weird. Ian likes to dominate Drake during the day. But by night . . . ?"

"Amanda, sexual domination is a common thing."

"It is?"

"I treat hundreds of powerful men who love it. Well, *treat* is not the right word. It's a matter of getting people to accept it and use it to release inner desires. I get dozens of Hollywood execs who have to make huge decisions involving millions of dollars every day. Greenlighting movies, dealing with childish stars, producers, and writer prima donnas. At the end of the day, these men want nothing more than to have a big man or woman shove a ball gag into their mouth, hood them, and tell them to shut up. They get to give up being in control all the time. Same with Ian. Very common. Hey, that would be a good idea to try in therapy!" she said, taking out her smartphone and making a note of it.

"All I know is that Drake's really strong."

"You don't have to be strong to poison someone, Amanda."

"Good point, Aurora. But you do have to have some muscles to strangle a person."

"Not if he's on drugs."

"Sure . . . And Aleksei blurted out that he and Drake have done autoerotic asphyxiation before."

"And that means what, Amanda?"

"I . . . ," I replied, stumbling. "It means that Aleksei thought they were doing a sexual thing and he let Drake do it willingly, not knowing it was going to be permanent. It would have been easy."

"So what's Drake's psychological motivation for icing both Aleksei and Keith?"

"The same as all the others: increasing his chances of winning the competition."

Aurora didn't seem impressed with my theory.

I added more: "Anger. Rage."

"At Ian?" she asked.

"It's misplaced, indirect, but yes. Ian, because he could ruin everything by leaving the money to an undiscovered heir. Rage at Keith for clogging everything up."

"But then every contestant could have killed Keith—and Aleksei—for the same reason: for getting in the way. Maybe we should stick to the psychological reasons, motivations from the psyche, so to speak. That's why you asked me here."

"True, true."

"Now, to recap with Drake, his motivation is perhaps that he has spent so much time running Ian's estate and life here. Not the money part, but the house, the grounds, the cars. Plus, I think he has a strong resentment for the other men since they are on the prissy side. I think Drake only respects men who ooze masculinity."

"Then why tolerate Ian, Aurora? He's not exactly macho."

"Money. Why else?"

"Correctamundo!"

"That's why most of the guys are here."

"Big surprise, Aurora."

"No, but Amanda, you have to understand why. Or at least, why the drive is so powerful."

"What's to understand? Money is alluring." I decided not to mention the thousands of dollars Drake had stored in the potting shed.

181

"But get inside the heads of these models. If they're successful like these guys are—or were—they live a very charmed life, despite the crazy lives they live. If we take out the long hours, the constant travel, the constant need to monitor their bodies and looks, we see that they wear expensive clothes, are surrounded by nice things, celebrities, fashion stars . . . it's an unrealistic life. But they know their careers are really short in modeling. That it can—and will—go away in an instant. So the money is a powerful cushion. Why do you think these guys are missing some of the big fashion shows in Europe? The spring/summer shows for next year are going on right now. They chose to be here because they have the onetime chance to have a very soft landing when it eventually comes. And for guys like Drake, whose modeling time has passed, and for Aleksei, whose career is teetering fast, this opportunity is as good as it gets. Yes, Ian's paunchy, obnoxious, and self-centered. But he won't be forever. See the attraction, Amanda? The desperation? The easy way out?"

"Okay, on that note, David Laurant?"

"David's an interesting one, Amanda. Ian loves his mischievousness, his refusal to feed into all the drama that's manufactured around here—including Ian's. Ian has a soft spot for David since he doesn't kiss up like all the rest. Despite the fact that he comes across as uncaring or arrogant, he's got a good shot at winning. He's a very, very good match for Ian."

"He doesn't come across *as* . . . he *is* arrogant and uncaring. But I have to agree, Aurora, I like that he doesn't feed on all the bullshit that's shoveled here. So, psychologically?"

"Just like all the rest, Amanda. I think he stays so cool it would be hard to tell how much he could resent someone like Keith or Aleksei. You saw his reaction when he found Keith dead. Either he is completely unaffected by emotion, or he was doing a hell of an acting job. It would take a complete sociopath to come downstairs after seeing Keith and go back to thumbing through a magazine."

"But you have to admit, Aurora, the ability to rein in emotions like that would make for a formidable killer. Perhaps he is a sociopath."

"Chilling, huh?"

"Okay, I was going to say Aleksei next, but that's a done deal. Keith too."

"I guess the only thing we could surmise is that Keith supplied drugs to Aleksei in the past. Aleksei looks like he was no longer clean when he died, and it looks like they were having sex the night Keith died."

"Well, they were either having sex or Keith went to Aleksei's room with his shirt off to deliver some drugs. In any case, that part of the case is closed. Okay, now we get to my favorite person, Gilles."

"He has a huge dick."

"That doesn't sound like a psychological reason, Aurora."

"No, but it's one of the reasons Ian likes him."

"Aurora, all the guys have huge dicks."

"How do you know?"

"I've seen them in swimsuits. The suits these guys wear don't hide a thing."

"I know," Aurora agreed. "They had to pixilate a lot of the bulges for airing on TV."

"Except for Marcus. Okay size cock, but the steroids have shrunk his balls to the size of pistachios. All sausage, no meatball in that sandwich."

"I like a good set of low-hanging balls, don't you, Amanda?"

Like a naughty schoolgirl, I replied, "Oh yeah. My ex had 'em. Loved 'em, but I could barely get them in my mouth sometimes."

"Isn't it great, us two girls talking smut like this? I mean, we're two straight women surrounded by gay men. There's no one to share our intimate thoughts with."

"You got that, sister," I said. Once again, I was liking Aurora more and more. "Now back to Gilles."

"Yes, Gilles. Classic narcissist. Walking onto the set completely nude!"

"Well, Aurora, it's one thing to have an inflated sense of self, but it's another to poison someone else."

"True, true. But the French mind can be so pragmatic about such things. A job to be done. Finished. Move on. But try and get a Frenchman to reach inside his head and reveal all, forget it. But they'll show you their cock in a moment's notice."

"So you haven't said if you think Gilles could have poisoned Keith."

"Yes. You heard him from day one. He wants to win and doesn't want any competition. In his mind, there isn't any. So eliminating one more person for a stake in Ian's fortune is just another business matter to be completed. No regrets. In some ways, he's the most chilling. His lack of empathy puts David in the shade because it's just like a steamroller propelled by an overwhelming desire to win, to inflate the ego while the true self suffers, withers. Hitler was like that."

"Okay. Let's get on to Ian's CEO, Lance Greenly."

"Who?"

"Lance. The one who looks like he's crying all the time. Receding hairline. Kinda plain."

"Oh, him. Yes, yes, I know about him, but I didn't know that was his name. Well, I can tell you one thing, he tolerates the boys that Ian is always letting into his bed. But I think that deep down, he really resents them."

"Enough to kill them?"

"Definitely. He works all the time. Day and night. Very passive-aggressive."

"Those are the types who end up killing. All that pent-up frustration. I don't know about you, Aurora, but if I worked that hard to keep a company afloat and I looked up and saw some himbo stepping to the front of Ian's gravy train, I'd be pissed."

"You'd have to be made of ice to let that go by."

"So you think Lance could kill just out of frustration? I mean, there's nothing in this whole setup that stands to benefit Lance. He's not even in the show."

"I think he would resent a possible heir, Amanda. Murder isn't always logical. The very act is illogical. Remember that revenge is a very powerful motive. It's not always about money."

"True, but money is a much better currency to spend than revenge. I mean, he is the only one who went down to the kitchen that night. Plus, you kill one person like Keith and the rage just pushes everything along by itself. Aleksei would be easy."

"So that's everyone," I added dejectedly.

"You didn't mention Ian."

"Ian?!" I remarked. "Aurora, why would you think Ian would kill his own son, then Aleksei?"

"I don't know, Amanda. I'm a psychologist, not a homicide detective. You've got to consider everybody. Why so glum?" she asked.

"I don't feel like I'm getting anywhere."

"Yes, you are, Amanda. You've discovered that just about everyone in the cast—and at Ian's company—is capable of having killed Keith."

"That's getting somewhere?"

"You know more than you did an hour ago."

"All I know is that someone went into the potting shed, got a container off the shelf, mixed gopher poison in Keith's cranberry juice, and the rest is history."

Aurora thought a minute. "You're sure of that?"

"Well, that's the theory, anyway."

"I'd say you're making quite a bit of headway if you came up with all of that yourself."

"I wish it was all of my idea, but the detective came up with a lot of it."

"So why is he letting you in on everything that's happening?"

"A guy I'm dating is a detective also, but he's out of town. So I think for Jerry, it's a misplaced camaraderie thing. Any friend of my boyfriend, Ken, is a friend of Jerry's."

"I see," she said, getting up to go. "Please keep me in the loop about what's happening and I'll be sure to let you know if I think of anything. And do be careful. There's a madman out there running around."

"Aurora, I have one last question I have to ask you." Aurora turned around and came up to me.

"And what is that?" she said, smiling sweetly.

"So who's out in front? Who's going to win?"

She grabbed my hand and squeezed it gently. "I'm not going to tell you that."

"It's Darryn, isn't it?" I asked, smiling like the Cheshire cat.

"Amanda, extraordinary looks and manners don't guarantee someone's going to win. The qualities I'm looking for are those that are a good match for Ian. Darryn's good qualities can get crushed by someone like Ian. After all, you don't throw a lamb into a cage with a lion."

"So what do you put in there instead?"

"A hyena," she replied, finally letting go of my hand.

"Oh, so it's back to David, Drake, and maybe Marcus, then?"

CHAPTER 25

Live Fast, Die Young, and Leave A Fashionably Dressed Corpse

I went out on the town that night. Again. After all, it was a Wednesday night . . . practically the weekend. I hit the usual places, all dressed up: Gucci two-pocket knit jacket, metallic tissue T-shirt, white linen stovepipe riding pants, and gold platform high-heel sandals. People didn't normally dress like this in Palm Springs since we were officially a resort and dress here was pretty casual. But I didn't want to blend in. I wanted people to see me. Notice me. And that wasn't going to happen with me wearing a T-shirt saying, PALM SPRINGS, I LOVE YOU; Levi's; and some flip-flops. Plus, the way I was dressed, when people asked me what I did for a living, I could honestly say I was on television and look the part.

At Aqua, I was having a conversation with three men whom I had passionately kissed in front of the other two, and still, they were vying for my affections. I was in the middle of telling a story about my television show when the worst person in the entire world walked into the bar: Jerry Hallander, the Palm Springs Police Detective of Homicide. The man was dangerous for me. I had the hots for him and he had them for me—an incendiary combination. I started wishing I had worn an old sweatshirt, striped jogging pants, and a dirty baseball cap with any shoes from Payless.

"Hi, Jerry!" I tried to exclaim, thinking that my excitement would cover up for my discomfort that of all the gin joints in all the towns in all the deserts, he walks into mine. I wanted him but was wracked with guilt about my feelings for Ken—even though we were only dating . . . a line I was getting tired of using to justify my dalliances. My three admirers gave up and drifted away, figuring that I had thrown them over.

"Amanda, what a surprise to see you here!"

And that's how it started, with two people acting like there was no attraction between them. We chatted for a while, had a drink or two, tried not to acknowledge the growing heat that was making the cool evening seem stifling.

"So . . . ?" Jerry said in that way that only made things more uncomfortable.

"Yes . . . well . . ." I replied.

Jerry took a deep breath, then spit it all out. "Amanda, you're an unbelievably attractive woman. Sexy, smart, Jesus!" he said, shaking his head.

"Yes, Jerry, I feel the same way," I said, knowing that it would only be a matter of an hour and I would be in bed with this very attractive, sexy man.

"You're attracted to me, I'm attracted to you. . . ."

"Yes, Jerry. Go on. . . ."

"I think we should . . ."

"Yes?"

He shook his head again vigorously, then was quiet for a minute. "Amanda, I can't do this. Ken is a good friend, a colleague. And you're dating him. If he ever found out that things got this far—even though we didn't do anything—it would destroy my friendship with him. And I don't think you want to betray him either. But you and I getting involved will not solve anything. In fact, it will only cloud the issue. I think the thing to do is for both of us to think again about what we're after, and to consider those around us who might be affected by actions we choose. I have to go now."

He took hold of my hand ever so gently and planted the tenderest kiss on my cheek, then walked out of the bar.

I wanted to cry. Was it because I was rejected? No, because I was acting like an asshole and it finally dawned on me as I saw my reflection in the mirror behind the bar. What had I become? I looked like a bimbo. A well-dressed one, but a horny woman craving attention from any male on two legs. Just then, my cell phone rang and I looked down at the caller's name: Ken Becker. I wanted to answer, but I was too ashamed of myself, so I pocketed my phone, paid for my last drink, and walked to my car alone.

I drove home in silence, turning off the radio when Patsy Cline's "Your Cheatin' Heart" started playing. I don't think I could have felt any lower than I did right then. I turned down my street, swung my car into my driveway and up into my mid-century carport, and turned off the ignition. It was late. I looked at my watch: 12:05 A.M. God, I couldn't take these long days anymore. I needed to get some rest and just wanted to undress, burn my clothes, scrub my soul, and go to bed, but I remembered that there were some house brochures in the trunk that I needed to take inside. I went and unlocked the kitchen door so I could carry the heavy box. Knucklehead was usually at the door, but he was probably sulking in my TV room, a result of my long days away from him. He had his doggie door in case he needed to go out and do his business, but when he was disappointed in me, he took his good ol' time coming to greet me, sniffing me casually, then looking at me as if I had hit him with a rolled-up newspaper. I waited a second. No Knucklehead.

I went back to the car. God, the brochures weighed a ton. I teetered back and forth with the heavy box on my towering heels. I know I should've taken them off when I unlocked the house, but I was so tired I only wanted to make one trip. As I neared the house, I could hear the tape on the bottom of the box ripping, sending 500 brochures cascading onto the dirty pavement. Great.

As I was about to let out a great sigh, I saw someone race up behind me, and the next thing I knew, that someone had something around my neck. I was being strangled. It happened so quickly I could hardly believe it was happening.

Next, I did what any red-blooded American female trained in karate would do: I forgot everything I ever learned. Almost. Instead of wasting time trying to get the rope off my neck (which is never any use since your attacker always has the element of surprise and the advantage of being behind you), I went right for his eyes. My assailant was wearing a ski mask or some sort of head covering, but I took my best guess and hit with my thumbs and index fingers, trying to gouge the eyes. I knew I only had ten to twenty seconds before I passed out, so I had to work fast and make my strikes count while I stabbed at my assailant's instep with my shoe's heels. We struggled back and forth, knocking over garbage cans, yard rakes, and pool floats as we smashed into just about everything in my carport. A second later, there was the sound of furious barking, growling, something ripping, and the rope around my neck fell away as I was shoved forward violently, falling over a garbage can and coming to rest lying on my back, staring at the ceiling of my carport while Knucklehead licked my face. A second later, I heard what sounded like gunshots going off, followed by silence. I checked myself for bullet holes but found nothing. I wasn't shot. My assailant was gone into the night. No sense chasing him now. Plus, I didn't want to mess up my Guccis any more than they were already.

A second later, Regina appeared standing over me, a gun in her hand.

"Amanda, I swear you have the lousiest dates of anyone I know."

It took me a few minutes to regain my composure. As I sat up amongst my smelly garbage, trash cans, garden tools, and gardening pots, I tried to piece together what just happened.

"You okay, honey?" Regina said, squatting down to talk to me at my level. "You had a close call."

"All those years of training in karate, and I couldn't think of a thing. I didn't even throw him over my shoulder, which I could've easily done. Damnit!"

"There's a big difference between a karate tournament and real life, sweetie. I remember when I was working on a picture with Richard Burton. He was so hammered, all those years of training and perfecting his craft didn't do him a lick of good in remembering his lines. They just wouldn't come to him."

"Regina, you do realize that you shoehorned that story into my comment about karate?"

"I think there's a great segue from your story to mine."

"Barely, Regina. As my nicer Lithuanian grandmother used to say, you can't put a Polish foot into a French shoe."

"I think I've just been insulted. But I don't speak Polish. Or French. Well, a little French . . . just the filthy words."

I shook my head to clear my thoughts. "So what happened here?"

"You tell me, Amanda."

"Well, I was taking this box of brochures into the house, when a guy in a ski mask ran up behind me and threw a rope around my neck and started strangling me."

"How did you know it was a guy?"

"I heard his voice, well, his grunting as he was trying to choke me. So you fired off a couple of shots at him?"

"Damn right!"

"You didn't hit him by any chance, did you?"

"They're blanks."

"They're loud enough. It's a wonder that the police haven't . . ." I tried to say, but was cut off by the sound of police sirens wailing in the distance, coming closer.

"Blanks or not, Regina, I'd put that gun away just for now. I don't think the cops would look too kindly on you firing that thing off in a city neighborhood."

"They do it all the time in Desert Hot Springs."

"That's because they kill people there. It's called drug gangs, Regina."

"Fine, have it your way."

Regina turned and tossed the handgun over the fence into her backyard, where it went off again with an impressively loud bang.

"Remind me not to do that again," she said.

"No argument there," I replied.

Chapter 26

You Have the Right to Remain Horny

The police arrived, guns drawn until we held up our hands and showed we were no threat. I gave a quick explanation of what just happened, minus the gunshots, so they would not only trust us, but so they wouldn't mess up the clear footprints left by my assailant in my garbage-covered garage floor, courtesy of the late-summer desert winds. As I looked over at Knucklehead, who was calmly taking everything in, I noticed he was standing on a piece of cloth that he must have torn from the leg of my attacker. That would explain the tearing sound I heard while Knucklehead was growling. I looked at it carefully while the police were calling for more units to arrive. Eureka! The cloth was very fine. I mean, very fine. It should be easy to trace this piece of fabric. I got my iPhone out of my purse and took a picture of the cloth since I would have to give it up for evidence. Knucklehead took a good chunk out the assailant's pant leg, because the piece was about three by four inches. Good boy! I called the policeman over and pointed to the piece of cloth. There must be samples of DNA on the cloth. The police came, took down our stories (Regina's being much more dramatic than mine, even though I was the one being strangled), photographed the scene, and to my delight, made two casts of the footprint. Jerry called and said he had two homicides tonight and could he please see me in the morning? He offered police protection, but I said I had another place to stay for the night. I had plans.

If you didn't count the dented garbage cans or the cop stationed out front for the night, no one would ever know that a life-and-death struggle had gone on right in my carport. Except for a few nosy neighbors, who occasionally peeped out of their curtained windows.

I called Ken first and told him all the details, having left out my meeting with Jerry earlier. He was worried about my safety, but I convinced him I could take care of myself. I told him I would stay at Alex's house since it was alarmed to the teeth and nearly impregnable. Plus, I would take my suddenly protective Knucklehead as my guardian. Then I called Alex, who was out of town climbing Thunderbolt Peak in the Sierras. I laid my trap and he fell right into it.

"Why don't you stay at my place for the time being?"

"Alex, that's so sweet. I hadn't even thought of that. It's been a long day, discovering Aleksei's corpse, investigating the potting shed, talking with Aurora, grocery shopping, and getting almost killed. I'm ready to pack it in for the day."

"You've got a key and you know the alarm . . . turn it on tonight. On another note, you're a smart woman, Amanda. Obviously someone in that house is worried that you're getting too close to the truth."

"Apparently."

"So what did you do today and yesterday?"

"Why a two-day timeframe?"

"Because if you're a killer and you're afraid someone is going to expose you, you're not going to wait days to strike. You're going to do it fast."

"Okay," I started, thinking about what I did the last twenty-four hours. "I got up, brushed my teeth . . ."

"No, not the stuff you did alone. Anything you did interacting with someone from Ian's house. E-mailing, telephoning, filming."

"I'll tell you the weirdest thing, Alex. As I was walking toward the potting shed, I could swear someone was following me."

"Did you see anyone?"

"No, not a thing. Just a creepy feeling that someone was watching me."

"Don't discount that feeling. Someone probably was there. Did Aurora give you any good clues?"

"Just the usual: anyone could have done it."

"Well, my dear Amanda, you better get packing and get over to my house. Set the alarm to 'home' so that it will go off instantly if anyone tries to get in a door or window."

"Okay, I will, Alex. And be careful tomorrow. Thunderbolt Peak is a really dangerous climb. I wish you and your team would tackle something easier."

"Amanda, life isn't worth living if you don't throw some challenges in there."

"Okay, Alex, you go take on a challenge. I'll stay here in Palm Springs and concentrate on living. Or trying to remain that way."

The next day, thankfully, there was no filming, but we would be working practically nonstop from now on to wrap up the series. Besides catching up on some real-estate work, I was supposed to sit down with Jerry and go through footage of Keith's memorial lunch, looking for clues.

I arrived at a local video studio to view the video and was escorted to a small booth where Jerry was sitting there with an editor.

"Hey, Amanda, good morning," he said as though the other night had never happened. Maybe it hadn't. I decided to play along. What choice did I have? Plus, it was better this way. I needed to figure out my relationship with Ken before I went out and confused the matter by adding Jerry to the mix.

"Good morning, Jerry."

"Amanda, this is Steve, our editor, who we can call on if we need him. He's cued up all the footage from the luncheon. Let me see here," he said, turning a control knob, which made a monitor in front of us come to life.

We watched as the guys insulted each other, ate food, and revealed dirty secrets about each other. Nothing out of the ordinary . . . at least for this crowd.

Jerry said, "Okay, so Drake is a sexual master to Ian and he's practiced autoerotic asphyxia with Aleksei before. And Aleksei ends up that night strangled with one of Drake's ties."

"You've confirmed that the tie belonged to Drake?"

"Yes, ma'am," Jerry answered. "Brooks Brothers."

"I guess that doesn't look good for Drake, does it?"

"I wouldn't hang the whole case on that fact, Amanda. Anyone could have gotten the tie out of Drake's room. Nobody seems to lock their doors at Casa Iffy."

"What about the cum on the floor in Aleksei's room?"

"Samples are at the lab."

"So we'll get results back Monday?" I asked eagerly.

"Amanda, this isn't *CSI*. It takes weeks to get results back from the lab in Riverside."

"Can't they move any faster? This is important!"

"Tell that to the Bureau of Forensic Services. Amanda, they've got hundreds of cases in front of my two samples."

"Two?" I asked.

"Aleksei's DNA and Keith's paternity DNA."

"You don't trust what Keith said . . . about Ian being his father?"

"I did some investigating, made some calls to Scotland, and a lot of what Keith claimed checks out. I'm just trying to be thorough. So that's what this remark from Aleksei about 'seeing them kissing was disgusting' is about?"

"Oh, they did a lot more than that, Jerry. They had sex."

"I heard."

"So?" I commented.

"What do you want me to do, arrest Ian?"

"No, it's not the fact that Ian had incest, but that he's not even remorseful about it."

"Again, Amanda, I can't arrest Ian for that. As for the rest of the secrets Aleksei spilled, infantilism with diapers, golden showers, enforced feminization, and pony play . . ."

I stopped Jerry by laying a hand on his. "What exactly is pony play?"

"Pony play is where guys dress up in outfits, usually leather, with masks and hoofs and everything, and act like ponies."

"Whhhyyyyy?" I asked.

"I think it has to do with the idea of being controlled. Being treated like an animal. Doggie play is the same thing."

"I thought doggie was where the one partner . . . never mind. Continue."

"So David is into enforced feminization . . . where he's *forced* to wear the clothes of a woman . . ."

"I know what enforced feminization is, Jerry. The point is whether having all these embarrassing sexual proclivities revealed to the world is enough to cause one of the guys to go ape shit and murder because of it."

"I really don't know, Amanda. This case has me stumped so far. The motive seems to keep moving around. Money, revenge, paternity, rage."

"One thing is certain, though, Jerry."

"What's that?"

"Palm Springs is anything but dull."

CHAPTER 27

Okay, You Can Open Your Eyes Now

I slept soundly that night. When I got up in the morning, I got my chance to do what I came to Alex's house for in the first place: snoop through his things. I wanted to see if his tales of "not seeing anyone special" were really true. They were. There were no pictures of new boyfriends in his clothing drawers, in his office, or the bathroom. And my photograph in a silver frame was still there on his bedside table that had the look that it was probably never moved, even when he brought a date home for the evening. Every time I came to his house, I always had to use the restroom so I could pass his bedroom and take a peek inside. I guess I was just looking for proof that we were soul mates. We still were. I just knew it was going to be a good day.

At 6 A.M., I drove over to Ian's house for another day of shooting. The plan was to start off with a quiet memorial service at Ian's house since Aleksei's parents had disowned him years ago for first being gay, then being a model, then getting hooked on crystal meth. I can see tough love with a son on crystal, but for being gay and a model? What can you expect from Christian fundamentalist parents living in Indiana? So much for forgiveness and acceptance.

The service was small and, of course, being taped for the show. The difference between Keith's and Aleksei's services was that this one was being held indoors, away from hawks. And to avoid tempting fate, there would be no releasing of doves this time. Ian did summon his guru Sai Baba Shu Baba again to collect another five thousand dollars and lead us in a prayer for Aleksei's soul so that it would transmutate or something into a tree or cow or merge with Shiva. I couldn't understand half the things the guru muttered.

We stood, holding hands in a circle in Ian's living room with our heads down for what seemed like an eternity. I kept staring down, noticing everything from the guru's shoes (this time, monk straps probably by Crockett & Jones or maybe Church's—I have to admit, the con man had great taste in shoes) to the other shoes in the cast, Drake's, David's, Ian's, Darryn's, then Aurora's. I didn't dare look up or around the room since the cameras were rolling. God, my neck was getting sore, I thought. How long can this guy go on chanting?

And then it hit me. Or rather, I saw it. Something I had seen somewhere else. And why it all bothered me from the moment I saw it. It was in front of me all the time. Staring me in the face and I missed it! I almost shouted, I was so excited about the possibility, but we had a whole day of shooting ahead of us. I could, however, slip out at lunch break since what I was looking for was right here on Ian's grounds.

We were supposed to be, in Jeremy's words, reaching the peak of the story arc, with the members of the show moving from "weakness to a place of strength," whatever that was. All I saw was bitchiness, territorial marking, tempers flaring, and Aurora keeping a scorecard at the end of each show. It was hard to tell who was winning, but the viewers' favorite was Darryn. Everyone loved Darryn, despite the fact that Aurora reiterated her belief that the winner had to be able to stand up to Ian's reprehensible qualities. But make no mistake about it, the show had shot into the stratosphere in the ratings category. And although the Q Channel cable network was eager for even more people to add the premium channel to their home lineup, millions of viewers were watching the episodes on the Q Channel's Web site, which was riddled with advertisements from some very happy companies. Then, during filming, Aurora announced that she was close to making a decision with Ian about the winner of the program. The timing was perfect, I thought.

We broke for lunch and I made my move. I went back out of the house, through the yard and directly to the potting shed, and went inside. This time, there was no creepy feeling of being followed or watched. There, on a bottom shelf was the one item that shouldn't have been there: the dented paint can. A dent in the side or, to be more precise, a crunch in the side. Even more telling were the two dents in the bottom—each approximately one-fourth of an inch in diameter. Dents created from the outside of the bucket, not the inside. Exactly three inches apart. They were extremely significant, but they didn't tell the whole story.

I put my find back on the shelf and went to my car to make a call to Detective Hallander where I wouldn't be overheard. I told him about my discovery and said that we needed to talk to Jeremy as soon as he was finished shooting this afternoon. I also said that we had a lot of work to do over the weekend. Early next week, during a show's taping, and just after the winner of the contest was announced, we would pounce.

I finished my call and as I was getting out of my car, I spotted a homeless man poking through the trash. Like so many of us, I normally move on after seeing them, and this only serves to make me feel guilty, since being invisible is the one thing they complain about the most. Anyway, something about this particular man struck me: He looked well dressed. Palm Springs has always had snappy dressers: Cary Grant, William Powell, and, ahem, Liberace, but our homeless have never made the pages of *GQ*. Something was wrong here, or actually, right here. There was a connection to the models in Ian's house somehow. I crossed the street and approached the gentleman. As I looked him up and down, I saw that at the bottom of his pant leg there was a piece torn out about the size Knucklehead had removed from the cuff of my assailant last night. Eureka! I was right: This was going to be a great day.

"Excuse me, sir. Please don't think I'm an asshole, but where did you get your clothes?"

"These?" he said, somewhat startled. "They're mine."

"Yes, I see. I was just wondering where you got them from? They're very nice . . . you look very nice. Snazzy," I said with complete discomfort.

"I got 'em from the fuckin' Armani boutique in Milan."

"I was just asking a question, sir, you don't have to be rude about it," I shot back, having screwed up my courage.

"You trying to have sex with me, lady?" he said, looking up at me. He then returned to pawing through and examining several empty bottles of men's cologne.

"No, I was just wondering what charity organization gave you those clothes."

He looked at me, exasperated. "No charity organization

gave me these, ya goddamned bitch. I found them in the Dumpster behind the Hyatt."

"You mean the Hyatt just down the street?"

"You know of any other Hyatts in town?" he sneered back.

Okay, easy now, Amanda. You're getting somewhere. He just doesn't like revealing his fashion sources.

"If you could give me those clothes, I'll . . ." I said, thinking fast, "see to it that you receive a lot more nice clothes."

"Get lost, you bitch, I'm not six years old. Give me more nice clothes! . . . Fuck! . . . You goddamn bitch!"

I was hit by a ray of light.

"Maybe this nice Mr. Jackson will help you change your mind," I said, pulling a twenty-dollar bill from my purse and waving it as if it left a scent wafting through the air toward starving noses.

"A twenty! What do you think it is, lady? 1940? I wanna see more than that if you want me to give up these fancy duds. This suit was made by Anderson & Sheppard, the best tailor in London."

"You know about them?" I asked.

"Yeah, I used to own four of their suits."

"Really?!"

"Yeah, I used to be a Realtor. Until things got bad."

"Shit. I'm about one commission check from joining you. But sir, please, I *really* need that suit!" I pleaded. I opened my purse and pulled eight more twenties and a fifty from my wallet. "Perhaps these will help. They'll help keep that lonely Mr. Jackson company . . ." I tried to say, but Mr. Charming had already snatched the group of bills from my hand.

"Cut the private-eye crap, bitch. Like I said, it's not 1940! I'll get out of these right now if you'll just leave me to my hunting and shut up about all the Dashiell Hammett shit."

And he took everything off right there, standing naked right in front of me as cars drove by and mothers struggled to cover the eyes of their children in the backseat. I wandered over to my car, popped the back hatch, and threw the clothes inside, vowing to have them dry-cleaned at least twice. I looked at the label: Anderson & Sheppard. Oh man, this was going to be easy, I thought. As I turned around, my homeless man had already pulled out a T-shirt and shorts from Ian's garbage and put them on. The T-shirt said, and I'm not kidding, GIORGIO ARMANI.

CHAPTER 28

A Pair Of Well-Fitted Trousers Can Be Very Revealing

We filmed all afternoon and into the evening. You could cut the excitement with a knife. The guys were all abuzz with the idea that the long ordeal of the show was about to end and one of them would be rich beyond belief. I had to admit that I was no longer sure who was going to be declared the winner. Viewers were confounded, too, as Jeremy had allowed the conflicts to die down and permitted the guys to get all warm and fuzzy—all part of his plan, or arc, as I should say. Jeremy was now looking for the *awww* factor. The fights and drama of the beginning episodes were there to get viewers to tune in. Now was the time to show "the strength of the characters." And it was working. The guys, turning from just plain disgusting to almost cuddly, whipsawed viewers' emotions, keeping them glued to their TVs or computers. People started asking themselves whether they judged the guys too harshly. After all, they now seemed like perfect gentlemen, well, after two deaths and Darryn's arrival. And then I understood why Jeremy had Darryn join the show out of the blue: The time was ready for the guys to undergo transformations. And change they did. You liked these characters now. You saw a soft, caring, vulnerable side that wasn't there before. The arc, again. Jeremy was playing us all like a Stradivarius. I had a newfound respect for him. He couldn't tell us about the change that was going to occur. It had to happen naturally, with Darryn as the catalyst in order to be real. Funny, in all this fakery, there was some reality.

This was all fine and dandy for the guys, but this change of plot had left me stranded. I could no longer be the wise-cracking fag hag, firing zingers from the safety of my bunker that I often occupied with Aurora. I now had to like these guys and, worse, show it. But lo and behold, I started to. I did see that underneath all the forced reality of the beginning of the series, there really were human beings there.

So why this big change of heart? Simple. I saw what the show had made me become . . . No, what I allowed myself to become. The show didn't actually make me do anything. I did it to myself. Celebrity went to my head. But I got over myself in the nick of time before I became a real asshole. So it was feelings of guilt, pride, and remorse that made me change course. Well, that and almost getting caught having an affair with Ken's best friend, and also taking a look in the mirror after months of barhopping and seeing Courtney Love staring back at me. If that's not enough to scare some sense into you, I don't know what will. We wrapped for the day at 8:30 P.M. I was dead tired. But I still wanted to take photos of the homeless man's suit and send them to Anderson & Sheppard before I went to bed. Jerry then could contact them in the middle of the night before they closed on Saturday afternoon their time. There was a lot of work to do tomorrow.

*   *   *

I met Jerry for breakfast to discuss our game plan for the day and weekend. We had to strike in a matter of days, so we had a lot of people to talk to, a lot of leads to investigate.

"I called Anderson & Sheppard at one A.M. and gave them a list of the guys on the show, including Ian and Lance Greenly, just to make sure."

"Lance spends some big bucks on clothes. It could have been him."

"They said they would look through their list of clients and would get back to me today. Do you know that besides suiting Fred Astaire and Gary Cooper, they made suits for Marlene Dietrich?"

"I knew that. That's why when I saw the label in the suit, I knew we'd have no trouble finding the owner. They're very, very high end, so very few men would be clients of theirs. Plus, they keep detailed records of their customers, besides their measurements."

"Oh, they said they got the pictures of the suit when they got in this morning. They wanted to impress upon you that they can replace the pants since they still have some cloth from that pattern left over. Isn't it wonderful that your attacker was wearing well-tailored pants?"

"My neighborhood has a very strict dress code for muggers, Jerry."

"Oh, I got the Chief of Police to put a rush on our DNA samples. We should have the results early Monday. And I talked to Jeremy last night on the phone."

"Did he reveal anything?"

"Certainly not the contest winner."

"I tried that already with Aurora. She's staying mum on that matter. So Jeremy wasn't able to shed any light on the murders?"

"No, he's ecstatic that the show is doing so well. And that it's about over.

"What about the footprint, Jerry. Of my mugger?"

"We weren't able to match it with any of the shoes belonging to the guys in the show. Ian and Lance Greenly included."

"But the suit showed up."

"But no shoes. I checked with the Hyatt. The Dumpster is emptied twice a week. If they were dumped in there with the suit, they're long gone. So the homeless guy didn't have nice shoes on when you got the suit?"

"No, he wasn't wearing any shoes. Oh well, it doesn't matter, Jerry. The suit ties one of the cast members to my attack. It's proof."

Jerry's phone rang. "I better get this. It's from overseas from the look of the phone number," he said, hitting the Answer button and putting the phone to his ear. "Detective Jerry Hallander here. Oh yes, thank you so much for calling back. You did? Noooooooo! Are you sure? . . . Yes, I'm sure you keep very detailed ledgers. Now, you're sure? Okay, I thank you for getting the answer to me so quickly and on such short notice. Thank you very much."

Jerry hung up the phone and stared at me.

"Yes? Jerry?" I said, snapping my fingers in front of his face to wake him from his trance.

"You're not going to believe this, Amanda."

"What?!" I asked, dying for the answer. "Who do the pants belong to?"

"What?" he asked, still in disbelief.

"I'm sorry, Jerry. That was grammatically incorrect. *To whom* do the pants belong?"

"Darryn Novolo."

* * *

By the time the shock wore off Jerry's face, I was smiling from ear to ear.

"I just can't believe it. I just can't," he repeated over and over.

"And why is that, Jerry?"

"First of all, he's seems like such a really nice guy. Not capable of harming a fly."

"And what's your second objection?"

"He wasn't even in town when Keith was murdered. I checked. He was just finishing a show for Prada in Paris. Hundreds of people saw him walk down the runway."

"I know that."

"So how do you explain it, then?"

Still smiling from ear to ear, I told him, "He had help."

"Who?"

"I'm not going to say quite yet. There are a few things I need to prove yet."

"But, Amanda, another innocent person could be killed while you're sleuthing around. This isn't Agatha Christie. This is real life. Someone could be in very serious danger!"

"I'm the only one in danger anymore, Jerry. The guys are fine now."

"How can you be so sure?"

"Because the threat to Ian's inheritance and the only witness who saw something he shouldn't have seen have been eliminated. And the odds are better now, with two contestants gone."

"I get Keith's death. Someone was worried that he might somehow have a stake in Ian's fortune, or at least that Ian might change his mind once he knew he had a son."

"Correct."

"And Aleksei's death?"

"Because of something he said."

"And you're not going to tell me that right now, are you?"

"No, but trust me. Just help me chase down some leads. When Aurora announces the winner of the contest, we'll have our own announcement to make."

The weekend sped by. Jerry dutifully made a lot of calls and hustled things along. Me, I made three important calls. One to Brian Hopper, celebrity gossip Web reporter. I had a simple question: Who does supermodel Darryn Novolo spend his time with when he's in Los Angeles? The answer didn't stun me, but it was unexpected nonetheless. I mean, I just couldn't picture the two of them together, but it bolstered my theory, making it bulletproof.

The second call was to Ken in Ohio. I filled him in on everything. He listened patiently, and after spilling everything I knew, he congratulated me on solving the case. I mean, he was really impressed and excited by what I had accomplished. And, oh, he missed me desperately. I told him I felt the same way. And he confessed he was horny. Me too, I said. Then Ken told me the best news of all: that he'd be back in two weeks. His mother was back home and getting around fine.

The third call was to Alex. In all the excitement, I realized I hadn't talked to him in a few days. He had summited Thunderbolt Peak and descended safely. Tomorrow afternoon, he would be heading back to Palm Springs.

Great, it was only Saturday afternoon and I had the rest of the weekend free. Free to nap and then plan on setting my trap.

CHAPTER 29

Colonel Mustard Was Blowing Professor Plum In The Library

Monday finally rolled around, the day we filmed the final episode. Or should I say night. Yes, Jeremy and the directors all decided that by filming outside around Ian's pool by torchlight, the announcement would have more drama. Everyone in the cast, the support people, and everyone who made the show happen—the cameramen, grips, electrical people—everyone was excited. Me too. But for a different reason.

The only change in our normal routine was that this one-hour episode was going to be very short in terms of filming. And most of it would be shot around Ian's pool by torchlight. The lead-up to the big announcement would be intercut with flashbacks of each contestant as they were highlighted for six minutes on this final episode. The purpose was, as Jeremy explained, to allow viewers to recap what had happened to each cast member over the course of the season and to keep them guessing as they tallied both the good and bad qualities of each contestant and how they reacted to stressful situations. The real reason was more pedestrian: to stretch out the episode so that advertisers would have more places to shove their commercials.

Before the cameras started rolling, Jeremy whipped the cast up into a frenzied state. "Well, guys, this is the day it happens . . . the day one of you will have his life change forever. I have five cameras to catch your emotions the minute the announcement is read. Now, I don't have to tell you that, no matter what Aurora and Ian's verdict is, I want big emotions. Big win! Big loss! Just make it big! And remember, you're under legal contract not to divulge the winner under any circumstances until the show airs. You got that?"

There was a murmur of agreement among the guys.

"And that goes for everyone on this set, has been on set at one time, or is in contact with anyone on this show."

And that was it. Even the threat of legal action didn't dampen the enthusiasm of us all that day. But it wasn't going to take a lot to stir up the energy, the guys were so wound up. Even David managed to show emotion. I was impressed. He had become quite the actor.

We all filed out to Ian's pool, which was decked out for the occasion with lots of torches and strategically placed uplighting. Since it was now late March, the nights were still chilly, but we went in short sleeves (and my cleavage showing—Jeremy's request) and pretended it was a balmy night.

Since all the flashbacks would be edited in later with Aurora's commentary on the ups and downs of each contestant, there was little to film. But Jeremy wasn't taking any chances. He hired a professional TV studio "cheerleader" to whip up the excitement the way they did before live-audience TV shows. I had to go along. It was like being at an Anthony Robbins life coaching rally. You knew it was all psychobabble New Age shysterism bullshit, but you had to join in jumping up and down, and yelling and clapping like an idiot because you would look like a sour grapes asshole if you didn't.

After twenty minutes, everyone was ready to burst an aorta, but we were excited and it showed for the cameras.

Aurora was ready.

"Gentlemen, we've all been through a lot together. I've seen you at your worst. And I've seen you at your best. Through it all, I've been watching and evaluating you, looking for that one man who will make a good match for Ian. That person needs strength, intelligence, courage, patience, and above all, a kind and giving heart. And after careful consideration of many, many months, I think that that man is"—she stopped, giving the cameras plenty of time to catch a variety of facial expressions—"Darryn Novolo!" she finished, holding a glass of champagne to the camera.

All cameras went to Darryn, who was really acting excited. Genuinely excited. The other guys were mortally disappointed—I could see it, knowing them all these weeks—but they did a damn good job hiding it.

And then I moved.

"There is another announcement to make," I shouted as I took center stage. All cameras swerved in my direction as Jerry bounded onto the set. I deferred to Jerry.

"Darryn Novolo, I am arresting you for the attempted murder of Amanda Thorne and the murder of Aleksei Kikorov!" he said, placing handcuffs on a dazed Darryn.

The cast thought it was all a planned joke. If they weren't standing with their mouths in a frozen laugh/startled expression on their face, then they were uttering a chorus of "What-the-fucks?" that would later be bleeped out.

"What is going on here?" Aurora asked. "I don't understand."

"Aurora, we have evidence that proves Darryn tried to murder me the night after Aleksei's memorial service."

"I don't believe it!" Aurora exclaimed. "It's not possible! Darryn, tell me this can't be true."

I turned on my biggest personality for the cameras, probably for the last time, and went for it. "It *is* true, Aurora. I'll start at the most recent developments, and we'll work our way back in time to reveal even more. As you all know, I was attacked by a strangler some time ago at my house. My dog managed to tear a portion of my attacker's pant leg off. The cloth was extremely well woven, but it would take weeks, maybe months, maybe never to find the company that made the pants. But lo and behold, a short time after that, I saw a homeless man going through Ian's garbage wearing a very fine suit. Guess what was missing from the end of the pant leg? A piece of cloth that matched the piece my dog had taken out of my attacker's leg. Coincidence? No. The homeless man found the entire suit in a Dumpster behind the Hyatt hotel, which is, coincidentally, just down the road from Ian's house. Just a few short blocks. Someone obviously wanted to get rid of the incriminating trousers and suit, so my attacker took them down the road and tossed them in the Dumpster, not realizing that homeless men frequent North Belardo Road because of the food handouts from the church on the corner. Bad planning. But also telling. Anyone who had spent enough time at Ian's house would know that. But one person was fairly new here: Darryn."

"So you're going to try and incriminate me on the basis that I don't know where the homeless get their food?"

"No, that realization that came into my head was just the icing on the cake. No, I'll let Detective Hallander tell about the pants."

Jerry, not having the great experience of being in front of a camera that I now had, cleared his throat and made a few false starts, but in no time, he rose to the occasion. "The label on the suit coat was from Anderson & Sheppard of London. We sent photographs to them, and thanks to the extensive records they keep of each client, we got a positive match: Darryn Novolo. Back to you, Amanda."

"Thank you, Jer . . . Detective Hallander. So was this the only foul play Darryn got involved in? Hardly. He also murdered Aleksei Kikorov."

Drake spoke up, "How can you be so sure?"

"We know the person who strangled Aleksei while he was sitting in his chair was tall. The tie that was used to kill him was tied around his neck and pulled up sharply to cut off his air and blood flow. So you're off the hook, Marcus," I said half-jokingly.

The cameras shifted to Marcus to catch his reaction. "Thank God," he said, wiping his brow with an imaginary handkerchief.

"Don't get too comfortable, Marcus. I said you're off the hook for Aleksei's murder. Not Keith's."

A trapped look flashed across Marcus's face.

"Allow me to continue. I think I was attacked because I was snooping around the potting shed where the poison that killed Keith was stored. But we'll get to that in a moment. So Aleksei's killer was tall. Aleksei, still sleeping off a drunken luncheon, was easy to approach from behind and strangle. But was there a way to make the murder look like an autoerotic accident? Yes. Sperm on the floor as if Aleksei was jerking off and the tie got too tight and he passed out and was strangled by his own hand. The only problem is, the sperm isn't Aleksei's. We got lab test results back late this morning that prove that the semen stains on the floor don't belong to Aleksei, but to Darryn."

"This is insane. I wasn't even in the U.S. when Keith was killed. I was in Paris."

I pointed at Darryn. "That you were, Darryn. At a fashion show in front of hundreds of people. So we have two murders that occurred at Ian's house. Unrelated killings from two different men trying to eliminate just about anyone to thin the ranks of competitors? It's possible, but I thought not. But the idea got me thinking. There were two murders. Most likely related, but that couldn't be carried out by the same person since one killer wasn't even in the country at the time of the first. So I thought, what if Darryn, our second murderer, had an accomplice? A lover perhaps?"

The guys in the cast, Lance, and even Ian looked very nervous all of a sudden.

I continued. I had everyone in the palm of my hand. "But who? I asked myself. Marcus, Drake, David, and yes, even Lance and even the producer of this show, Jeremy Collins, could have committed the first murder. And of course we're assuming that the reason Keith was killed was because he revealed on an episode of *Things Are a Bit Iffy* that he was Ian's long-lost son. The cast members had every reason to bump off Keith since he might cause Ian to divert a lot of money to a man if he thought he was his son.

"Lance Greenly," I started, watching a rather shocked Lance step back into the shadows off camera, "could have done it because of the same reason, fueled by resentment that he had worked so hard over the years and now it could all be given to someone who shows up at the last moment. It could even be the show's producer, Jeremy. Why? Ratings, my dear. People in Hollywood would kill for high ratings. And maybe in this case, someone did."

David, who usually had plenty to say, finally spoke up, "Amanda, you know I like you. But this all seems so insane. It's too unbelievable. It's surreal!"

"At first, I thought so, too, David. So who committed the first murder, of Keith? Killed by strychnine in gopher poison from the garden shed. The police had been all through the shed but didn't find the container used to mix the poison. But there was one item in there that, when I first saw it, well, it didn't seem right."

"What do you mean, wasn't right?" Drake asked, the one person most tightly connected to the shed.

"It hit me the day you wanted to throw out a wineglass Aleksei had chipped. Ian claimed he couldn't see any damage, but you insisted on throwing it away."

"So what does that have to do with something that shouldn't have been there?" Drake asked, puzzled.

"Drake, face it—you're so obsessive, I'm surprised that you don't catalog your turds. Anyway, in the first place, the pail was dented on the side."

"Yeah, and I would have thrown it away. . . ."

"Exactly, Drake. But it was there the morning of Keith's murder. There was no time to throw it away."

Drake the Dominator started to emerge. "Are you accusing me of mixing poison in the pail to kill Keith?"

"Not to mix poison in, Drake. *To stand on.* You see, ever since I really looked at the pail, there was something strange about it: It was crunched on the side. So I asked myself, why would that be? It was used by a painter to hold paint when painting a wall, or touching up here and there. So why the dent on the side? Then I noticed something even stranger: two small, round dents on the bottom. Were the two related? They were. It came to me when we were praying last week in our little mini-memorial service for Aleksei. I was looking down at the soft pine floors in Ian's house. There, in the shiny polyurethane finish were small dents. Dents caused by high heels. Shoes worn by Aurora Cleft!"

Aurora was flabbergasted. "Amanda, this is preposterous! Why would I kill Keith? I have nothing to gain."

"That's what I thought initially when I was searching for who stood to gain the most from Keith's death. It wasn't you. So I searched around, but the arrow pointed to all the rest of the cast. What finally clinched it was what Aleksei said in a drunken ramble at Keith's memorial luncheon."

"And what was that?" Aurora asked haughtily.

"Well, I can't slur my words as well as Aleksei did, but he said something to the effect that he had hot gossip. He saw two people kissing, and that it not only shocked him, but that it was disgusting. Why would Aleksei think that two people kissing were disgusting in a house full of gay men? Naturally, everyone assumed he was talking about Ian kissing Keith, who was his son. Incest. But it wasn't. Aleksei was a notorious heterophobe. He hated seeing straight sex, so what he was describing was you, Aurora, kissing Darryn!"

"This is madness," Aurora sputtered. "It's all conjecture."

"The answer is actually much simpler. You see, Aurora, you are Ian's therapist. Some time ago, Ian told you he had incurable pancreatic cancer. You are also Jeremy Collins's therapist—a fact that you lied about when we talked at the Mexican restaurant. Anyway, this got you thinking. Jeremy was looking for a big idea for a show and you supplied him with it: *Things Are a Bit Iffy*. You told him about Ian's cancer, the former boyfriends, and before you knew it, there was a program with a whopper of a premise. You selected the former boyfriends for the program, including your ace card: Darryn Novolo, a complete newbie to Ian and everyone else. You'd let the show start, let the contestants destroy each other and make each other look bad, then introduce Darryn, your lover, and he'd be suave, kind, and likable. It would be so easy, until Keith threw a monkey wrench into the works by saying he was Ian's son. Well, he had to go. Having a bedroom on the far side of the house gave you the opportunity to move around the house and grounds fairly unnoticed. So you knew that Keith had a glass of cranberry juice before bedtime, and that afternoon you slipped in the potting shed, got the dented pail, and turned it upside down in order to reach the gopher poison on the top shelf. But in standing on the pail, you left two dents from your Christian Louboutin heels in the bottom and you slightly crushed the pail because of your weight. You mixed the poison there and carried it into the house where you put it in Keith's cranberry juice, knowing that he was the only person in the house to drink it. End of Keith. When Aleksei opened his mouth and said he saw the two of you kissing, he had to go too. But this time, you decided that Darryn would do the job and you would make height a clue that would put you in the clear."

I took a long swig from a glass of wine and continued, "When you helped me carry Aleksei upstairs to his room after he passed out at Keith's memorial luncheon, you knew that we left him in a high-backed wing chair. There was always a chance that he might wake up, so you advised Darryn to come up from behind him and strangle him with a tie that one of you had stolen from Drake's room. Then Darryn put some crystal meth on the top of the dresser, forced some up Aleksei's nose to make it look like he had snorted it, and jerked off on the floor to make it look like he was practicing autoerotic asphyxiation. You even suggested as much when you came up to join the rest of us. But you made another fatal mistake with a comment you made."

"What comment, Amanda?" she snorted.

"After you made some sort of remark about 'who could be doing this,' you directed our attention to the drugs on the top of the tall dresser."

"And what's so wrong with that? There *were* drugs there."

"Yes, Aurora, there were. But *you* couldn't see them because of your height. I wasn't allowing anyone into the room, and *I* could barely see them on top of the tall dresser. You only knew they were there because Darryn had just told you where he left them. That's why both of you were at the back of the group looking into Aleksei's room—you were going over the details of what to say and do downstairs before you came up and joined us."

One more swig of wine. God, you really get dehydrated solving crimes.

"All it took was one phone call to the right gossip Internet reporter in Hollywood and he told me that you were seen with Darryn when he was in town. The connection was made. The reason Brian Hopper didn't report the two of you was because he couldn't believe you were straight, Darryn. He wanted to be sure of his story."

Darryn looked up at all of us, then glared at Aurora. "I'm not. I'm gay."

Aurora flew across the room, her fists wailing at Darryn while policemen tried to pry her off him. They managed to handcuff her, and as they were leading her away, Darryn lobbed one more Molotov cocktail onto the pyre.

"I wanted the money, Aurora needed a good-looking model, and I pretended to be straight for her."

I shrugged my shoulders. "I guess that psychiatrists can be in denial too."

CHAPTER 30

Amanda Becomes the Butt of A Joke

The dust eventually settled. The final episode aired to huge ratings, Aurora and Darryn were in jail awaiting trial, and the final winner of the competition for Ian's affections . . . ahem . . . the money . . . was in doubt. Since Aurora's opinion on who should be the final winner was somewhat tainted, Ian and a team of lawyers from the network and his own personal cadre of attorneys hammered out an agreement and Ian chose David Laurant as his boyfriend to the end. This, of course, led to more publicity, which pleased the network and Jeremy Collins, whose career was on a trajectory that would make a rocket jealous. And life returned to normal, whatever that was.

Ken had successfully gotten his mother back on her feet and returned to Palm Springs just in time for summer. He and I cooked a wonderful dinner and as we sat in my dining room, Knucklehead asleep at my feet, he asked the question that I was dreading, because once he asked it, I wasn't quite sure how to answer. Should I be completely honest about my dating, even though I never gave away any more than a passionate kiss? Should I stretch the truth just a bit, or should I be a conniving, thieving liar?

"So, besides the show, the celebrity, and two murders, did you do anything exciting while I was gone?" he asked with complete and total innocence.

"Naw, nothing much. Just the same old stuff," I replied, hoping that the acting skills I had honed while on *Things Are a Bit Iffy* would help me cover my guilt. And while I expected the long arm of the law to come down from the sky and reprimand me (or at least point a finger at me accusingly), Ken cut another slice from his filet and ate it without a hint of doubt of my story crossing his face. And that was it. Had I carried off the perfect crime? Ken was a very good detective, and I was sure he heard things about me while he was gone. But his face, his emotions, and his questions signaled that he was willing to accept my answer completely and without reservations. I felt like a louse for a while but justified my behavior by saying it was the fame that made me do it.

While I had escaped being made accountable for my actions with Ken, I had to face a much tougher adversary: Alex.

He wanted to deliver a gift to celebrate my stint on television, so I invited him over for dinner at my place. I had since toned down my wardrobe, no longer needing to be noticed all the time. Just like beauty, fame is fleeting. So I greeted Alex at the door in Levi 511's, a white button-down oxford-cloth shirt—and a pair of zebra-print Maud Frizon loafers. Hey, I might have come down from my once-lofty pedestal, but I was going to wear nice shoes after the descent.

He showed up carrying a huge rectangular object covered in wrapping paper with a huge red ribbon and bow perched on the corner of the object. It was a painting or photograph judging from the shape as he ferried it into my living room and set it gently on the floor.

"Open it," he said, grinning from ear to ear.

I tore the paper off and took a look at the enormous photo. It was a picture of an asshole. A human asshole.

"Do you like it?" he asked eagerly.

"What's not to like? It's a four-by-four-foot picture of an anus."

"Five-by-five," Alex corrected me.

"Even better. There's nothing better for filling up empty wall space."

"But do you like it? It's the one that our ex-client Vicktor Teller sent us on our cell phones."

"Oh, I remember. It made me lose my shit on national television. Alex, it really is beautiful. What did you do? Photo-manipulate it?"

"Photoshopped it myself, and had it enlarged and re-touched. Then I added special effects and false colorization, removed the hair, etcetera," he said proudly.

I had to admit it, the photo really *was* beautiful. It didn't actually look like an asshole. It looked like a beautiful red–orange crater. But there was a much bigger question that formed in my head: Was this just a piece of art for my home, or was it a message from Alex to remind me of what I almost turned into? Neither me nor Lady Gaga could see through his poker face, so I resigned myself that it would always be both: art with a message.

"I'm going to hang it right there near the entrance," I said, pointing toward my front door.

"Great idea. I was going to suggest that. Perfect location."

I got up and carried the photo over to its new home and

set it down on the floor. Alex and I stood there for a moment, not a word passing between us, but volumes of unspoken words being exchanged. He then walked over and gave me a big hug—a hug I really needed right now since I was on the verge of tears.

"Welcome back," he said.

We sat down to eat and we had a wonderful, wonderful meal. And I had never felt more real.

Epilogue

Eleven months after the final episode of *Things Are a Bit Iffy* aired to a huge viewership, Ian Forbes died peacefully in his sleep at a hospital in Los Angeles with David Laurant at his side. David sold Ian's huge estate in Palm Springs with Amanda Thorne and Alexander Thorne as listing agents. Because of the controversy surrounding the winner of the wildly popular *Things Are a Bit Iffy,* David Laurant gave $2 million each to Drake Whittemore, Marcus Blade, and Gilles Moreau. David Laurant eventually moved to Paris where he lives to this day. And the paternity tests conducted on Keith MacGregor proved conclusively that Keith could not have been Ian Forbes's son. Evidence showed that while Keith was Ena Forbes's son, genetically he could not have been fathered by Ian Forbes. The results of this test were made available to Ian at around the time he chose David Laurant as his companion and heir from the television show that made them both very famous. For a short time.